The man w...
confidence...

Rachel found herself wanting to know what the combination could produce between the sheets, and as she watched Marc study the room, her mind took off in a sensual fantasy that had her squirming in her seat.

Her pulse quickened as she mentally traced a finger over that sharp jaw. She could practically feel his early evening stubble scraping against her skin. She wondered what those lips tasted like. Did he kiss hard or linger softly?

But just as her fantasy reel started getting to the good stuff, that steamy gaze swept back and collided with hers.

For the briefest moment, he perked, one eyebrow arching slightly and his mouth revealing the barest hint of a smile. It disappeared quickly, but it was enough to give her a jolt of tickling pleasure. Every instinct told her he was as attracted to her as she was to him, and she stored that tidbit away for safe keeping.

Marc made purposeful strides toward their table. She caught the uneven blink of his eyes and faint glance to her chest before he cleared his throat and turned his attention to his brother.

Oh, yeah. This little stay of hers just might end up being a lot of fun....

Dear Reader,

A favorite romance hero is that deliciously enticing bad boy. You know the one—the rebel with a wild side, the misunderstood loner with a bad reputation and a good heart. Readers love their stories and writers love writing them. But I couldn't help but wonder, what about the bad girls? Can they be as worthy of love and redemption as their ever-so-handsome counterparts?

That was the thought that led to the story of Rachel Winston. She's a privileged woman who has come to realize that money and looks alone can't make a person whole. She's searching for value and purpose. And with the help of a few new friends and a strong delectable hero, she gets all that and love, too!

I hope you enjoy Rachel's story as much as I enjoyed writing it. Please drop me a note and tell me what you think of it at www.LoriBorrill.com.

Happy reading!

Lori Borrill

Lori Borrill

INDISCRETIONS

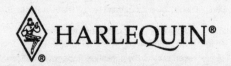

TORONTO • NEW YORK • LONDON
AMSTERDAM • PARIS • SYDNEY • HAMBURG
STOCKHOLM • ATHENS • TOKYO • MILAN • MADRID
PRAGUE • WARSAW • BUDAPEST • AUCKLAND

Recycling programs
for this product may
not exist in your area.

ISBN-13: 978-0-373-79552-9

INDISCRETIONS

ABOUT THE AUTHOR

An Oregon native, Lori Borrill moved to the Bay Area just out of high school and has been a transplanted Californian ever since. Her weekdays are spent at the insurance company where's she's been employed for more than twenty years, and she credits her writing career to the unending help and support she receives from her husband and real-life hero. When not sitting in front of a computer, she can usually be found at the baseball field playing proud parent to their son. She'd love to hear from readers and can be reached through her Web site at www.LoriBorrill.com.

Books by Lori Borrill

HARLEQUIN BLAZE
308—PRIVATE CONFESSIONS
344—UNDERNEATH IT ALL*
392—PUTTING IT TO THE TEST
430—UNLEASHED
484—THE PERSONAL TOUCH

*Million Dollar Secrets

For Al and Tommy

1

CAMERAS STARTED SNAPPING the moment the jet-black Bentley rolled into view, shutters popping off like rounds of machine-gun fire from the army of paparazzi that had gathered on the grounds of the Clearwater Springs Resort. Behind the Bentley, four black SUVs followed in procession, turning off the highway and onto the long drive that would bring them up the hill.

It looked like the fricking president was arriving instead of a spoiled and pampered heiress, and Marc Strauss ground his teeth as the fiasco began to unfold.

Reporters who had perched themselves near the large iron gates shot their last photos and were now rushing to reposition, charging through the meticulously manicured flower beds and bounding over the low stone walls. They ran around like savages, smashing plants and smearing mud, scaling the metal sculptures that had cost Marc a fortune. It was everything he could do to keep from pushing through the glass lobby doors and personally extricating each and every one of them from his beloved property. Instead, he clenched his fists and directed his anger to the person responsible.

"This is a damn circus," he said to his brother, Brett. "The cleanup is coming directly out of your salary."

Brett smiled and watched the scene as if this was the most exciting day of his life. "No problem, bro. I'll just take it off all the money we're gonna make from this publicity." He slapped Marc on the back and pointed to the caravan. "That guest right there is going to put Clearwater Springs on the map."

Marc opened his mouth to say they were already on the map, that they didn't need Hollywood's latest princess to drum up business, that the debacle that was Rachel Winston and her shiny new criminal record would turn away more loyal clients than it would bring new ones, but they'd gone down that road before. Marc had made his arguments and had ended up giving in to Brett's marketing scheme—mostly because the deal had been all but done before Marc had heard anything about it.

It was only now, with the tranquility of his resort obliterated and the stampede of reporters decimating the world he'd so carefully built, that he realized what a mistake that had been.

"Ease up, Brother Grim," Brett said, snapping his gum and winking off the chaos as the Bentley rolled to a stop in the circular drive. "Once she's inside, security will escort our unwanted guests off the property." He waved a hand over the scene. "We'll get Cory out here to clean up the grounds…"

The sound of Brett's voice trailed off as the chauffeur opened the back door of the Bentley and the woman who would be their ward for the next thirty days stepped onto the stone drive. Marc had seen pictures of Rachel Winston. Heck, everyone had. And they'd seen plenty of her after she'd done the spread for *Hush* magazine last year. In the photos she was beautiful—distractingly so—with a china-doll face, dark, silky hair and exotic blue eyes. Now Marc knew that beauty wasn't digitally added after the shoot.

She was the real deal. And as he watched her greet the crowd with a poised and tentative smile, his annoyance withered under a sudden ray of lust.

He swallowed hard as she smoothed her hands over her slacks and adjusted her shirt. Her conservative blue pants and pale pink blouse shouldn't have been sexy, but they were. Accessorized with pointy-toed heels, a pink clutch purse and wide-framed sunglasses, she oozed high-end Hollywood. And that was no wonder. Perfection had been literally bred into her DNA when her handsome studio executive father crossed genes with Hollywood's hottest starlet of the seventies. Though the marriage between Richard Winston and Abigail Moore had been brief and turbulent, it had lasted long enough to produce this striking creature, and as a member of the opposite sex, Marc had to give them a nod. Rachel Winston was the thing hot dreams were made of. Toss in a colorful history and a bad-girl image and it was no surprise that the world ate her up.

"I wonder if *Hush* let her keep that yellow fuzzy thing," he heard his brother say. "You know the picture I'm talking about?"

Know it? The photo had been emblazoned on Marc's brain from the moment Brett dropped the magazine on his desk two weeks ago. Sprawled across a brown velvet chaise, she'd been clad in a pale lemon bra, one strap hanging haphazardly off her shoulder as she held a finger to her lips and eyed the camera with a sinister stare. Her dark, wavy hair had been mussed, her makeup slightly smudged to give the impression she'd been busy—doing what was left for the reader to imagine. And though, at the age of thirty-four, Marc considered himself an evolved and liberated man, one look into those sapphire-blue eyes and his imagination had taken off with all the tact of a hard and horny teen.

Brett had unearthed the photo spread as one in a series of ploys to get Marc to buy into this arrangement, and Marc hated to admit it had worked. One glimpse of Rachel Winston in all that glorious flesh and a tow truck couldn't have dragged his eyes from the photo. That sexy gaze stuck a hook in him that had taken days to shake off.

And now she was standing on the steps of his resort, just as alluring and electrifying as she'd been in those photos. Except now she was here for real.

God, he was in trouble.

"I wonder if she brought it," Brett added. "That or that blue sparkly thing she was—"

"She's our charge, not a play toy," Marc snapped.

The reminder was spouted as much for his own sake as his brother's. Given the situation, he didn't need the flutter in his gut or any encouragement from the peanut gallery. Keeping his resort in one piece through the next four weeks would be hell enough. Marc couldn't afford to make pals with their celebrity guest. That position was already taken by Brett, and if one of them didn't keep his wits about him, Ms. Winston would be running this show before the week was out.

Sooner, if this grand entrance of hers was any indication.

A somewhat feminine-looking man stepped out of one of the SUVs and began barking orders to the others. Several men took aim at the paparazzi, backing the bolder ones off and creating a clear path from the

Bentley to the lobby doors. Suitcases began lining up against the caravan, and while Marc wanted to go tell the woman she wouldn't need much more than a maid's uniform, he gestured instead to the bellmen to begin helping with the luggage.

The men grinned and rushed out with expediency Marc hadn't thought them capable of. And in the corner of Marc's eye, he noticed all the other lobby staff poised and fitted as if this were inspection day at an army boot camp.

Great, just great. Rachel Winston hadn't even walked in the door yet and already she was handling the reins. This would be worse than he expected. He mentally began plotting his discussions with all the parties involved, laying down the ground rules as to what was expected and who would and wouldn't be running the show for the next thirty days.

Starting with Rachel and her father.

Marc had a number of clarifications to make with them, undoing the misconceptions he knew his brother had laid down—the first one being that Rachel would most definitely be *working* during her stay. She'd been sentenced by a judge to work thirty days as a maid as punishment for a battery conviction she'd obtained when she'd injured a hotel employee down in San Diego. After a string of minor tussles with the law, a judge apparently decided a little empathy might be what the incorrigible rich girl needed.

And Brett had somehow arranged to have her sentence carried out here in their resort, no doubt by making a number of promises Marc had no intention of honoring.

Rachel Winston was here to work, and the sooner

he made that clear, the sooner they could get this over with.

He half expected she might high-tail it out the second she discovered this wouldn't be the covert vacation Brett had promised. And if she did, that would be fine by Marc. He'd only agreed to this when Brett assured him there would be no misunderstandings between all parties, and today was the day to make sure that was true.

So when Richard Winston emerged from the Bentley and stepped to his daughter's side, Marc decided it was time to get this meeting over with. If the new guest was going to end up leaving, best it happen quickly.

RACHEL PERKED UP after getting her first glimpse of Clearwater Springs. Leave it to her father to arrange an absolutely perfect place to carry out her sentence. The resort was upscale and secluded, tucked in the desert south of Palm Springs. Close enough to attract the big-city clientele, but far enough from the usual resort spots to offer the privacy she needed.

As she stood by the car and waited for her father, she mused that he really was at his best when rescuing damsels. She wondered if this had become the definition of their relationship; she created messes and her father swept in as her caretaker, lavishing her with attention and proving, once again, that he would always be there for her no matter what she did. Maybe underneath the confident woman she portrayed was a scared, insecure child who needed to continually test the loyalties of everyone around her.

It wouldn't be a stretch. With both parents having spent their lives putting their careers ahead of her, any good therapist would understand why she was forever throwing herself in a spotlight to capture their attention.

Instead, she decided she was overanalyzing things. In reality, she'd grown up just as independent as her famous mom and dad, and she didn't need a crisis to prove that they loved her. Unfortunately, there was no convenient daddy complex that would excuse the fact that she was basically a screwup. As much as she'd like to find a golden pass, twenty-six was too old to blame anyone but herself for her problems. And even though she'd said it before, this time she really did intend to pull her life together, accept those things she couldn't control, and make a plan for what she could.

And looking around these lush grounds and to the desert mountains beyond, this resort was the perfect sanctuary in which to do just that.

"See?" her father said as he rounded the Bentley and stepped to her side. "I told you it was beautiful."

"Perfect," she admitted. "Brochures usually exaggerate things, but in this case, apparently not."

He squeezed her hand. "You've got nothing to worry about."

Rachel smiled and nodded, even though she hadn't been worried. She'd suffered worse than this. And really, how hard could it be working as a maid for four little weeks? As long as the job didn't involve numbers or heavy reading, she could handle it just fine. And when she wasn't on the job, there was plenty of quiet scenery for the reflection and meditation she hoped to take in during her stay.

As long as she didn't spend it flanked by all these reporters.

"Rachel, have you ever cleaned toilets before?" yelled a woman she recognized from one of the L.A. dailies.

Cameras flashed to catch her reaction.

"Do you expect the staff will be friendly after what you did to that poor woman at the Four Seasons?" yelled another.

Questions came at her from every direction, regurgitations of the same thing they'd been tossing since the incident at the hotel six months ago. Further back, if she counted all the other times she'd thrown herself into the public eye.

She knew they'd go away if she only stopped feeding them material, and the older she got, the more she realized that was exactly what she wanted. Trying to find a place in the world she grew up in had been an unequivocal disaster. She hadn't her mother's talent nor her father's smarts. And though Hollywood had accepted her on looks alone, the business of capitalizing on her failures ultimately proved a more profitable arrangement.

What she wanted now was to slink away from all this. Maybe move to Paris or Milan, out of the public eye like a number of celebrities she knew, and…do what?

That was always the question.

Do what?

"Hey, Rachel, pose for a picture," one reporter called out, a scrub brush in one hand and a pair of yellow rubber gloves in the other. He apparently thought she might don them and smile for the camera, and as ludicrous as that seemed, she realized she'd done more ridiculous things before.

Her father pointed a finger and one of his burly bull dogs disappeared into the crowd, taking the brazen reporter with him.

"Let's get inside," he said. But before they could take a step, they were greeted by two men.

Correction, one man and one…Adonis.

The sexy stud extended a hand to her father. "Richard Winston, I'm Marc Strauss."

His voice sang in her ears, rich as milk chocolate, as he uttered polite greetings. He was tall, taller than many of her father's entourage, and he held himself with a calm authority that seemed to dominate the space around them.

"You've been speaking with my brother, Brett," the man added, gesturing to the shorter blond at his side.

Both men were striking, blessed with similar square jaws and long, straight noses. But it was the eyes that set them apart. Brett's were friendly and blue, while Marc's…why, they were piercing. Serious and assessing. The kind that could strike a weaker man down. And when he turned that gaze on her, she literally felt it touch her skin.

"Ms. Winston, it's my pleasure," he said, holding out a hand while he waited for her to take it.

She bit her lip, unable to unlock her grip on that striking dark stare, and when she placed her hand in his, a pulse of electricity made her shiver. He must have felt it, too, because those steely eyes—blue-gray, she now realized—registered the slightest hint of shock.

Swallowing, he casually pulled the hand away and made way for his brother, who seemed more genuinely pleased and eager to meet her. But despite the charm and affection pouring from Brett, she couldn't drag her attention from Marc.

Rachel wasn't a stranger to handsome men. They were a dime a dozen in her social circle. But never had she run across one so instantaneously captivating. He wore a dark navy-blue suit, tailored well to reveal a fit body underneath, trim and long, but not lanky. A silver

blue tie lay against his white shirt, polishing off an ensemble that was all business, right down to his black
oxfords and tidy black hair.

Without thinking, her eyes whipped to his left hand
where the sight of a bare wedding finger left her tickled.
It filled her head with all kinds of ideas. All of them
bad, most likely, but no one had said an affair was off-
limits. And barring any pesky girlfriends, it seemed she
could only improve her situation by cozying up to the
management.

"After you," he said, gesturing toward the door. "I'd
like to clear our uninvited friends out of here before our
regular guests are disturbed."

She sensed a grain of annoyance in his tone, one Brett
apparently didn't share since he kept grinning at the
cameras as they made their way to the door. It left her
curious, and she began to wonder whose arrangement
this was. Had she been forced upon them by the owner
of this hotel? Did these men owe her dad a favor? The
court had left it to her father to arrange a place to serve
her sentence. She'd assumed everyone was in agreement,
but now she was beginning to have doubts.

It would be nice to know what she was walking into,
but in classic fashion, her father kept his dealings on a
need-to-know basis. Even when those dealings were her
life for the next thirty days.

It's not your concern.

She could already hear him say it. *Business matters,
honey, nothing for you to involve yourself in.*

Whenever she tried to inject herself into an important
discussion, he'd all but stop short of saying, *Just be quiet
and look pretty.* And she knew without a doubt that
very phrase had tumbled to the edge of his lips more
than once in her life. But he also knew she was her

mother's daughter. Giving orders only meant she'd do the opposite, and just as he'd learned to deal with Abigail, he'd learned to treat Rachel with the same guarded caution.

Taking a breath and exhaling the thought, she stepped into the relative quiet of the lobby.

Let go of those things you can't control.

A very wise and spiritual friend had provided her that mantra, and she silently repeated it as she took in the surroundings.

The Clearwater Springs Resort was a compound of tan stucco buildings with clay tile roofs, built in the Spanish mission style common to the area. Rustic furnishings of dark wood and rich textiles took up the grand lobby. Overhead, elaborate iron chandeliers hung from an exposed beam ceiling, the chunky wood clean but aged as though ancient wars had been fought in that very room. The space was a strange mix of upscale elegance and unrefined charm, the cold stucco walls softened by warm yellow light, fine regional art and polished terracotta floors.

Apparently, there would be little sacrifice to her accustomed lifestyle while spending a month on these grounds. Aside, of course, from the forty hours a week she'd spend cleaning rooms. Although, even that was in question, judging by a few offhand comments her father had made on the ride up.

Stefan, her personal assistant, came to her side, a key card in one hand and a pile of papers in the other.

"You're in the Hacienda Suite," he said, handing her the card.

"But—" Brett said, turning to Marc, who quickly cut him off.

"It's the best we have available," Marc snapped.

Brett narrowed his eyes, but kept quiet. Yes, there was definitely a dynamic in this room, and as soon as her father took off back to L.A., she intended to get to the bottom of it.

"I'll start unpacking your things," Stefan went on, oblivious to the undercurrent swimming around them. "When you're ready, give me a buzz and I'll show you where we're staying."

"We?" Marc asked, obviously not expecting the additional guest.

"Stefan is Rachel's assistant. She needs him," her father interjected. Then he turned to Brett. "That was part of the agreement."

The look on Marc's face soured. "Yes, well, if the four of us could sit for a moment and chat, I'd like to discuss that agreement." He motioned toward a large wooden door.

"Of course," her father said. "Rachel, why don't you go with Stefan while I talk to these men?"

She pressed her lips and tried to fight off the embarrassment that threatened to color her cheeks. She didn't know why her father's brush-off hit her so squarely. He'd been treating her like a child since she was one. But for some reason, dismissing her in front of Marc packed an additional sting.

"If it pertains to me, I'd like to be there," she said.

"Sweetheart," her father started, but Brett cut in.

"Actually, there's a log she'll need to complete for the courts. I'd prefer we go over it with both of you."

Defeated, her father sighed and checked his watch. "Fine, as long as we're brief. I need to be in Santa Barbara by six."

"This won't take long," Marc said, tossing another one of those icy glances to his brother.

And as she followed the men into the room, she couldn't shake the feeling that her stay at Clearwater Springs was going to end up far more interesting than she'd expected. Though interesting good or interesting bad, it was way too soon to tell.

2

MARC ESCORTED Brett and the Winstons into one of the conference rooms that opened to the main lobby, gesturing toward the large mahogany conference table in the center of the room.

"This is a nice resort you've got here," Richard said. He held a chair for Rachel then took the one beside her. "My assistant wasn't kidding when she said this was quite the hidden gem."

"Thank you," Marc said. "We're just beginning to build a name for ourselves."

"You two co-own this place. New blood in the hospitality industry, if I recall."

Marc looked forward to the day he could answer that question with a yes. Though this resort was his home and career, he was still far from being able to call it his own. But if things went as planned, that day would eventually come.

"The resort's owned by a partnership," he admitted. "Brett and I are managing general partners."

Richard smiled. "It's a lovely resort." He turned to Rachel. "It looks like you'll have plenty to do while you're here."

"Absolutely," she said. She turned her eyes to Marc. "I can think of a number of things, already."

He didn't miss the innuendo in her voice or the suggestion in those dark, seductive eyes. A blade of heat curled up his neck, tightening his collar and drying his throat as she held that gaze on him and curved her mouth into a playful half smile.

"You mentioned something about forms," Richard added. "I really do need to make this quick."

Brett opened his binder. "I got these from your office. They were sent by the court. I just want to clarify the process of logging Rachel's service hours so there are no misunderstandings."

"Actually," Marc cut in, darting his gaze from Rachel and grabbing quick hold of his wits before this meeting took off without him. He placed a hand on the papers Brett was about to slide across the table. "There are a few other things I'd like to clarify before we get to that." Swallowing hard, he pushed his thoughts to the business at hand. "It seems most of the discussions have gone on between Brett and your staff. Now that we're all here together, I'd like to make sure we're in agreement over the expectations by the court as well as yourselves."

He eyed his brother, pleased to find no panic in Brett's eyes. Maybe he really had made sure it was clear Rachel would be expected to work during her stay, and that over the next four weeks, she'd be considered an employee, not a guest.

"Of course," Richard agreed.

Marc opened his mouth to begin when the door opened and his concierge popped in.

"I'm sorry to interrupt," the woman said. "Phil Arnall is on the phone. He says he needs to speak with you immediately."

"I'll have to call him back," Marc said.

"I told him you were in a meeting. He insists I interrupt. Plans to wait on the phone until you pick up." The woman smiled apologetically. "He's not taking no for an answer."

"Sounds like my kinda guy," Richard joked with a laugh.

Only Marc wasn't laughing. Phil was one of the shareholders in the property who sat on the board of directors. Though the man owned a small fraction of the resort, he was responsible for one hundred percent of Marc's headaches, continually looking for problems that didn't exist, and Marc yearned for the day he and Brett owned controlling interest. He'd give anything to be able to tell Phil to go to hell.

Unfortunately, the man had a talent for inciting the other partners, and as long as the board had ultimate power to call the shots, Marc had to keep peace.

Exhaling an angry sigh, he rose from the table.

"I'm sorry, I'll have to take this." He turned to Brett. "You know what we wanted to cover."

"Not a problem," Brett said, but Marc held his eyes on his brother for a pause in an effort to convey this was serious.

While he and Brett worked well together, it was no secret that Brett was the sales and idea man and Marc was the organizer and voice of reason. Together they created a successful balance, working in unison to temper each other's extremes. But left alone, Brett Strauss was a loose cannon, and without Marc around to periodically defuse, only bad things happened.

"I said, not a problem," Brett repeated. And with a nod, Marc felt satisfied enough to walk out and take the call.

He stepped down the hall to his office and picked up his private line. "Phil, I'm in the middle of a meeting. I hope this is urgent."

The comment was futile. Phil considered everything urgent. If only Marc had known that before accepting the man's money back when they'd been wheeling and dealing to buy the resort.

"What am I looking at on television, Marc?" Phil asked.

"I haven't a clue."

"It looks like my hotel has been converted into a celebrity halfway house. I don't remember you clearing this with the board."

My hotel. An overexaggeration at best, and though Marc should be accustomed to the man by now, the phrase still rattled his nerves.

Clearwater Springs was Marc's brainchild. As long as he could remember, he'd wanted to own and operate a resort. When he was a kid on vacation in Maui or Palm Springs, he'd fantasized about coming to a place like this and staying for good. And as soon as he'd graduated from college with majors in finance and hotel management, that was exactly what he'd set out to do.

With the help of Brett's career as a professional tennis player and parents with wealthy connections, he'd scraped together a partnership to buy Clearwater Springs. And as part of the long-term plan, his family would continue to buy out the others' shares until they held controlling interest.

Marc had spent the past ten years working to buy this resort, and if things continued to go as planned, it would only be a few more years before he owned it outright. But in the meantime, he was stuck having to calm the waters with a retired bank executive who had too much time on his hands.

"I don't need to clear any employees or guests with the board," he said. "You know that."

"You've entered an agreement with the San Diego courts. All contracts need to be approved—"

"There's no contract, Phil. Ms. Winston is free to carry out her sentence at any hotel or resort she chooses. The arrangements surrounding her stay are all within the power Brett and I hold as managing general partners."

Phil huffed. "You should have run this by us. If this turns out badly, you could ruin our investment and the reputation of the resort. I think this is too much publicity too soon. We don't yet have the reputation to withstand any bad press that might come out of this."

"I can hardly see what—"

"I don't like it. I don't like it one bit. Are you aware of that woman's reputation? I don't care how much money she has, that's not the kind of clientele we want to attract to Clearwater Springs. Next, you'll have a flock of drunken rock stars checking in and trashing all the rooms."

Marc rolled his eyes. "Only the good rooms, Phil."

Marc's meaning flew over Phil's head. "This is a family resort. You'd sold us on that concept yourself."

"And it still is a family resort. Nothing's changed."

"You better hope it doesn't. I'll be keeping a close eye on the financials." *He always did.* "If business goes in the tank over this I'll have you tossed. That we *can* do."

It was a line Marc had heard a dozen times before, and each time it never failed to give him a headache. Granted, he could have probably avoided Phil's uproar if they'd sent a communication to the board. But in heart and soul, Clearwater Springs belonged to Marc. It was his life and passion and he treated it as such.

"I understand your concerns and assure you, you have nothing to worry about."

He went on to recite the same pacifying speech he always gave when Phil called with his butt in a bundle. By the time he got off the phone, more than twenty minutes had passed and a glance outside the window found the Bentley and the entourage gone.

Great.

Unless Rachel left with them, the only thing between Marc and a dozen more headaches was his faith that his brother had sufficiently laid down the ground rules.

And knowing Brett the way Marc did, that kind of faith was in short supply.

"DON'T WORRY. You aren't going to have to do a thing," Brett assured, taking a swig of his iced tea as he, Rachel and Stefan enjoyed drinks on the shady terrace.

They'd just said goodbyes to Rachel's father, who gave her a quick kiss and a promise to come back and visit in a couple weeks. It was a sweet offer, one Rachel knew he sincerely meant. But if the man actually showed his face there again, she'd donate her entire trust fund to charity. Her dad wasn't coming back. She'd be lucky to get a quick phone call, which was all fine and good. From the sound of things, she was going to have her hands full as it was.

"We're pairing you with Anita," Brett went on. "You'll like her. The day crew has gone home for the day, but I'll introduce you to her and Jolie, the head of housekeeping, tomorrow. But mostly, you and Anita will work together. She'll handle the dirty work. You can help by doing a bit of dusting." Brett shrugged. "I'm sure you'll be more bored than overworked."

"That might be a good time for you to phone in your daily blog," Stefan said.

With a fresh honeydew margarita in one hand, Stefan jotted down a note in the planner that kept both him and Rachel organized. Or more accurately, the planner kept Stefan organized, Stefan organized Rachel.

He'd been in her employ practically since she graduated high school. At first, she'd been put off by the idea of an assistant, feeling as though her parents had basically hired a babysitter. But it wasn't long before Rachel realized how badly she needed someone like him to handle her affairs.

It was after she'd convinced herself that she was a horrible student that Rachel was diagnosed with a severe form of dyslexia. She was terrible with numbers, and despite the tutoring her parents had hired, she still couldn't read without effort. Having Stefan come into her life had been like receiving a new, smarter brain, and she'd quickly decided that life without him would be unconscionable.

Unfortunately, his relationship with his partner, Tyler, was growing serious, and lately he'd been cutting back his hours. She'd practically had to beg him to come for this four-week stay, but with many of her friends brushing her off since her conviction, she needed him now more than ever.

"And vacuuming," Brett added. "You can do that, right?"

Rachel shrugged. "I don't know. We've always had people…"

She trailed off when she saw Marc step onto the terrace. He'd removed his jacket and tie since she'd seen him last, and while she'd loved the tailored suit look, she liked this casual style better. Without the jacket, she could see he was bulkier than she'd first assumed. He'd rolled his sleeves up to his elbows and loosened the top button on his shirt, revealing a faint tuft of dark hair that disappeared to places she wouldn't mind exploring. His bulging chest and biceps couldn't be hidden despite the loose fabric, and as she trailed her eyes down his flat stomach, she wondered what other delectable surprises the man kept hidden under those clothes.

Wouldn't it be fun to find out?

Heck, right now, she'd settle for a better view of his butt, but he remained in the archway facing the tables as he scanned the crowd.

Despite the fact that Brett and Stefan were still talking, Rachel couldn't rip her gaze from the sexy stud. The man was a cocktail of calm confidence and hot intensity that left her dizzy with intrigue. She'd love to know what that combination could produce between the sheets, and as she watched him study the room, her mind took off in a sensual fantasy that had her squirming in her seat.

Her pulse quickened as she mentally traced a finger over that sharp jaw. She could practically feel his early evening stubble scraping against her skin. She wondered what those lips tasted like. Did he kiss hard or linger softly? Would he groan or would the only sound be the heavy beat of her heart?

She felt as though she could sit and stare all day, mentally feasting on that body until her blood simmered to the boiling point. But just as her fantasy reel started getting to the good stuff, that steamy gaze swept back and collided with hers.

For the briefest moment, he perked, one eyebrow

arching slightly and his mouth revealing the barest hint of a smile. It disappeared quickly, but it was enough to give her a jolt of tickling pleasure. Every instinct told her he was as attracted to her as she was to him, and she stored that tidbit away for safekeeping. Brett assumed she'd be bored during her stay. Not if she had her way with his brother, she wouldn't.

Marc made purposeful strides toward their table, her mouth getting drier as he neared, and when he approached and uttered a greeting, she took a casual sip from her straw before offering her most flirty hello.

She caught the uneven blink of his eyes and faint glance to her chest before he cleared his throat and turned his attention to his brother.

Oh, yeah. Attraction with a capital *A* on a road that ran both ways. This little stay of hers just might end up to be a lot of fun.

"I guess I've missed Richard," he said, not yet motioning to take the available seat at the table.

Brett nodded. "Yeah, we're just going over the details now. I've mentioned that we're pairing her with Anita, went over a few of the things she'll be doing." He gestured to the chair. "Sit down. Have a drink."

To Rachel's pleasure, he took the seat and ordered coffee from the waiter.

"And how did your discussion go after I left?" Marc asked. "Are we all clear on the expectations?"

"Yeah, yeah," Brett said absently.

The comment left Rachel confused. She didn't know what Marc was referring to, since after he'd left the conference room, there was no discussion other than how happy they were to have her.

"What expectations, exactly?" she asked.

Marc turned those dark steely eyes to hers. "That this is a job and a responsibility, not a vacation."

The cynical tone should have offended, but instead she grew more intrigued. As much as Rachel loved hot men, she loved a sexual challenge even better.

She blinked innocently. "Does that mean I can't use the pool?"

"Girl, we're paying for the room," Stefan injected. "You can use anything you want."

But her gaze never left Marc's, and the table went quiet as she awaited his answer.

A fire in his eyes brimmed. "The standard shift is eight hours with a one-hour lunch. During that time, I'm expecting you to conduct yourself as an employee. What you do before and after is your business, as long as it's not disruptive to the other guests."

She studied him, hoping to read from his expression what kind of options she had for "after," but he remained silent and professional. Possibly oblivious to her signals, but probably not. Instead, she suspected inside that handsome head he was waging war with his libido. And the fact that he could be working hard to keep his distance only excited her more.

She'd spent a lifetime brushing off advances from eager men and, in the end, most were either after her body, her money or an avenue to her father. Oh, how she'd love the opportunity for a hunt more challenging than shooting tigers in a cage.

"I can work an eight-hour day," she said. She took another sip of her margarita.

Brett nervously tapped a finger to his drink. "Cool. Anita works Monday through Friday, eight to five."

"Uh, that's going to be a problem." Stefan thumbed through his planner. "Tuesdays are her spa days. I'd switch it to the weekend, but Gwendolyn couldn't possibly make it up here on a Saturday, and Sundays are blocked out for reflection and meditation."

Marc's eyebrows shot up.

"So, we'll find someone she can work with on Saturdays," Brett said. "And housekeeping has all kinds of project work that won't require supervision, like cleaning mirrors—"

"Nothing with perfumes or chemicals," Stefan said. "She's deathly allergic."

"Everything they do involves perfumes and chemicals," Marc snapped. "It's housecleaning, for crying out loud."

Stefan shook his head and flipped to a blank page. "Another issue we'll have to deal with. I know of a good supplier who offers hypoallergenic cleaning supplies. I'll get you the information. They should be able to overnight a supply."

The fire brimming in Marc's eyes ignited. "We aren't ordering anything. You need something special you get it at your own cost."

"To clean *your* hotel?" Stefan scoffed.

"Why don't I try what they've got and we'll go from there?" Rachel suggested, hoping to avoid a fight. Besides, she wasn't even sure she was allergic to anything. Once, three years ago, she'd developed a rash after cleaning a compact with window cleaner. Ever since then, Stefan had insisted she was sensitive to chemicals.

Stefan sighed and shook his head. "Fine, if you want to risk it. But when you swell up and turn orange like an Oompa Loompa, don't say I didn't try." He scribbled another note on his pad. "Marty will be here day after tomorrow to go over Rachel's special diet needs.

Can you give me a contact in the kitchen he can work with?"

Now Marc's neck began to flush. "We have an award-winning staff and chefs that can handle any special diet needs. What they can't handle are extra people in the kitchen telling them what to do. Tell *Marty* he can fax the specifics to the resort. There won't be any meetings."

Then he turned to his brother. "You were supposed to have gone over this with Richard. I'm not having this resort turned into a circus."

"We're not asking for anything a standard high-end facility wouldn't provide their guests," Stefan quipped, clearly in an effort to snub Marc and his hotel.

And it worked. Marc looked as if he was one more prod away from bounding over the table and going for Stefan's jugular.

"You know," she attempted. "It's been a long day and I don't know about you, but I'm tired." She pulled Stefan's planner away and closed the book. "I've had enough business for one day. Maybe these discussions would be easier after a nice meal and a good night's sleep."

Just then, Marc's cell phone rang. Taking a heavy breath, he rose from the table. "I need to take this. Your idea is a good one. Let's meet in my office tomorrow at nine."

Stefan reached for the planner, but Rachel held him off. "Tomorrow at nine will be perfect."

And with that, Marc stormed off, leaving the three of them staring at each other.

Brett was the first to speak. "Look, don't worry about my brother. We'll get you what you need. In fact, it would be a good idea if you ran everything through me.

I'll have a talk with him and we'll cancel this meeting tomorrow—"

"No." Rachel held up a hand. "I'd like to meet with him tomorrow. Alone."

"Rachel," Stefan warned. "I hope you're not thinking what I think you're thinking."

She smiled and sipped the last of her drink. "I'm thinking the next four weeks will go much more smoothly if I extend an olive branch to Mr. Strauss. And I can do that much better without an audience."

"As long as you aren't dangling a hot pink thong on the end of it."

Brett choked on his tea, and Rachel chuckled. "Does your brother have a girlfriend?" she asked as casually as she could pull off.

"Marc?" Brett laughed. "He's deeply devoted to Clearwater Springs. No other woman can compare."

She tried to conceal her pleasure, but Stefan knew her too well. "Don't even think about seducing that man. I've got enough problems as it is."

And she could certainly relieve one of them if she got Marc Strauss to come play in her sandbox. Though Rachel had a very short list of things she was good at, handling men was right there at the top. With everyone else working so hard to make sure this sentence of hers went as painlessly as possible, getting Marc on their side would be the least she could do. And a lot of fun in the process. Because, no matter how angry he seemed just now, she hadn't the slightest doubt that the bulk of that gnarly exterior came from the fact that he was torn between what his body wanted and his judgment wouldn't allow. And once she convinced him that his body knew best, they could all start getting along.

"Nine o'clock tomorrow," she said to Brett and Stefan. "You boys sit that one out."

3

MARC CHECKED HIS WATCH. Ten minutes after nine.
Rachel and Stefan were fashionably late, of course. He
would have expected it of them, but Brett was usually
more prompt.

Leaning back in his chair, he rubbed his hands over
his face and tried to brush the sleep from his eyes. It had
been a long and restless night, the events of the day before playing over and over in his head like a bad horror
film. Reporters ransacking the grounds, Stefan and his
demands, Phil Arnall threatening to pull the rug from
under him. The scenes had flashed through his thoughts
for hours, growing brighter and more threatening as the
night wore on.

And in the middle of it all was Rachel. She'd left
him staring at the ceiling for a whole slew of reasons
all her own—the most notable being a dose of lust that
only seemed to compound as time went on. Every time
his mind had settled toward the peace of slumber, she'd
come at him in his dreams, all tender flesh and wanton
eyes. She'd placed his hands on her breasts and her lips
on his, the sweet taste of that honeydew margarita just
as vivid as if she'd really been there in his bed.

She'd flashed that pouty smile, the one she'd offered from the brown velvet chaise. Damn Brett for throwing that magazine on his desk. It had been haunting him ever since, and now that he had the real woman to complete the fantasy, he hadn't been able to shake it from his thoughts.

But he had to find a way. This situation had too much potential for blowing up in his face. Though he hadn't wanted to admit it to Phil, the man had been right on one account. The resort was still in its infancy, and he and Brett were still proving themselves. This wasn't the time to make any major mistakes, especially not when the risks were more than his alone.

He sighed at the sight of his empty office. This was no doubt a precursor to the level of commitment he could expect from Rachel in the coming weeks. And while he couldn't control her, he could definitely control the reports he provided to her parole officer.

Abandoning any notion that this meeting would take place, he rose to go find his head of housekeeping. But when he opened the door to his office, he found Rachel standing there, one fist raised as though she'd been about to knock.

"Going somewhere?" she asked.

He backed up two steps. "I, uh…"

It took only a glance at her coy, playful smile for him to forget what he'd been doing. And what red-blooded male could blame him? The woman was beautiful. There was simply no other word for it. And today she was even more breathtaking than she'd been the day before.

He blinked as she stepped into his office, those hips swaying gracefully under the thin film of her dress. Dotted with pale blue flowers, the silky summer slip hugged what little it covered, leaving only the most intimate body parts up to the imagination.

And what it did show was pure bliss.

She'd let her dark, wavy hair hang down around her bare shoulders. Her makeup was pale, leaving her looking more fresh than made up. Complemented by a touch of sweet perfume, she came at him through all the senses, and his only defense was to swallow hard and retreat back to his desk.

"I thought you'd forgotten our meeting," he managed to choke out once he had his back to her.

"And miss a chance to spend my morning with you?" she asked. "I don't think so."

Flattery. He'd love to say it wouldn't work, but damn, it did.

He took his seat, working hard to keep his priorities on his career and out of his pants.

"Is Stefan coming?" he asked.

She shook her head and lowered to one of the two chairs facing his desk. "No. Actually, I asked the others to leave this meeting between you and me." She smiled sweetly. "I thought we might make more headway if you and I could talk alone."

He certainly loved the idea of dumping the annoying assistant, but the two of them alone with very little between his hands and her naked body didn't sit well.

It would if you'd pull your mind out of her skirt.

"I can't shake the feeling we're getting off on the wrong foot," she said. "I'd like to start over. Maybe see if you and I can come to an understanding…or something."

"Or something," he muttered.

She flashed a girlish pout. "Sometimes, I think you

don't like me at all." Then she curved it into a smile. "Other times, I think you like me very, very much."

The temperature in the room seemed to shoot up— probably from the steam pouring through those big blue eyes—and he struggled to avoid getting sucked into the siren's web.

This isn't worth all you've worked for, he told himself, dragging his attention away from all that glory and onto what really mattered to him the most.

Clearing his throat and shifting in his seat, he looked out the window to the resort he loved so much, reminding himself of all the hopes and expectations he had for his future. Every one of them in jeopardy if he didn't keep his head about him.

"It's not that I don't like you," he finally said. "If you'd come as a guest, I'd welcome you and your entourage with open arms, ordering the staff to make your stay as enjoyable as possible." He turned his gaze back to hers. "But you aren't here as a guest. You're here as a ward of the court, and our duty is to a court order that says you're here to work."

"I wouldn't expect anything less."

"Good. Because everyone's watching. I've done my best to keep the media off the grounds, but you know as well as I some are getting through. And I can't prevent the staff from talking. I don't know if you're aware of this, but your parole officer called last week. She wanted to clarify the work you're supposed to be doing here. And before she hung up the phone, she left me with a polite but firm reminder of all the things this resort could be cited for if we should be found falsifying documents or otherwise misleading them about what you're doing here."

He paused to let that sink in before adding, "I've

worked hard to get where I am. I'm not going to jeop-
ardize it."

"I understand completely."

She rose and moved to his side, leaning a hip on his
desk and crooking her foot on the seat of his chair. The
satiny hem of her dress inched up, exposing one smooth,
delicious thigh.

He tried not to look, but his traitorous eyes betrayed
him. They took in every bare, luxurious inch from the
drape of that flowery fabric down to the dainty toes that
peeked out from her blue sandals. His mouth watered,
aching for a taste of her, and he pondered how easy it
would be to slide his fingers up that skirt and grasp a
handful of silky flesh.

"And what better way to make sure this all goes
smoothly than to keep a close eye on me?" she asked.

She trailed a finger along the inside of his thigh,
stopping short of his growing erection before turning
and heading back toward his knee.

"You see," she said, lowering her voice to just above
a whisper. "I think we could form a partnership that's
mutually rewarding. One that starts with these lips—"
She touched her lips. "Right about here."

Slipping her foot off the chair, she leaned in and
pressed her mouth to his, proving in an instant that every
fantasy he'd had about her had been elementary compared to the real thing.

The touch of her lips was even softer, the taste
sweeter, her body firmer. She ran her hands up his chest
and slipped onto his lap, and when she opened her mouth
and prodded her tongue toward his, he realized his only
choice was surrender.

His body whipped to life, the blood rushing through
his veins double speed. He sucked in a breath as his

hands skimmed up her torso, snaking along the slippery fabric all the while ignoring the desperate warnings in his head. He wanted to stop, needed to fend her off, but his body wouldn't obey his orders. His hands simply kept roaming, his tongue probing, his hips jutting forward in an attempt to get his cock closer to the place it begged to go.

"You're so hot," she groaned into his mouth, turning him hard as steel. Long ribbons of her dark hair tickled against his neck as she slipped her fingers up over his chin and trailed them along his jaw. She guided his mouth over hers, the soft twirling of tongues increasing in speed until they grew hot and devouring. His hungry hands found those breasts and he nearly lost his manhood, the supple mounds so glorious in their perfection he could barely decide where to start.

It stunned him, the power she had over him. The way smooth heat turned to raging fire at the simple press of her lips. He could only imagine the devastation of taking her fully, bare flesh to bare flesh, the two of them out of this office and in the comfort of his apartment. It was only when he started to plan it that his senses eked through the mist and began to take hold.

What was he going to do, carry her through the lobby? Even acting covertly, all eyes would be on them. He didn't need a mirror to know they had sex written all over them. The stiff bulge in his pants alone would draw eyes. And as the reality of the situation settled further, hot lust turned to angry fire.

Pushing her off him, he rose and stepped away. "That's enough," he said, taking a few more paces toward the window to walk off some of his idiocy.

What the hell was he thinking?

And more to the point, what the hell was she trying to pull?

"Come on," she urged. "You can't stop now."

"I should have never started, and I assure you, that won't happen again."

She shot out a breathy laugh. "Why? Are you gay?"

Sarcasm. That was good. It fueled his anger and doused any remnant desire.

He stepped to her and grabbed her forearm, intending to escort her to the door, but first he had some words to share.

"I'm not gay, nor am I interested in playing games or forming partnerships. You're here to work. And if that's not part of your plan, you can waltz that pretty little butt of yours to a new hotel."

She snatched her arm from his grasp and huffed.

"I don't know exactly what you did to land in this mess," he went on. "I don't follow the tabloids and I really don't care. But I do know one thing. The judge had something in mind when he sentenced you to this. Maybe he wanted you to come down from your ivory tower and see how real people lived—people with jobs and families and responsibilities. People with hopes and dreams and aspirations. Who don't treat the world like their playground and everyone in it their toys."

She placed her hands on her hips and gasped, but it only angered him more.

"Yeah, that's right. Someone's telling it to you straight for a change."

"You don't know anything about me."

"No, but what I've seen so far isn't impressive." He raised a finger to her chest. "You've got an opportunity here to step into someone else's shoes. To see how life is for people who don't have the world handed to them on a silver platter. And if you weren't so spoiled and afraid, you might actually get something out of it."

"I'm not afraid of anything," she said defensively.

"Then prove it. Do the job you've been sent here to do. Stop worrying about what day you can have your nails done and start thinking about what it's like to earn a living the hard way. Maybe in the process, you'll discover the joy of real accomplishment."

She raised a hand to slap him but he grabbed her wrist midair. "I wouldn't do that if I were you."

"You ass!"

She waited for him to deny it, to argue or scold some more. And when he didn't she snatched her hand from his grip, turned and stormed out the door, leaving Marc hot and furious—and all be damned, aroused.

Moving back to his desk, he collapsed in his chair and placed his head in his hands. He had no idea what he'd just done. She'd pushed too many buttons and in the midst of it he'd snapped, rattling off a load of bias and assumptions he wasn't even sure had merit. Rachel had been right. He didn't know anything about her other than what he'd caught through hearsay and rumor. For all he knew, he could have been completely off base and owing her an apology.

But his gut told him he'd hit the nail on the head. He could see it in her eyes, just as he could see in her eyes that no one had ever talked to her that way before. He'd stormed down a road never traveled, and where it led, he had no idea.

He only knew for certain that somewhere in all this, the repercussions wouldn't be good.

RACHEL RACED TOWARD HER SUITE, holding back tears that she wasn't sure were from anger, hurt or humiliation.

Maybe a mix of all three. She only knew for sure that she didn't want to be here. She wanted to be back at home, in the safety of her estate, among friends and family and people who cared. Not here with that ogre who had the nerve to fondle her body then toss her aside like trash.

Rushing out of the main building, she stepped into the warm morning sun and sucked in the scent of clean air, every bitter word of Marc's running through her head while his kiss still lingered on her lips.

How dare he presume to know her? How dare he presume to know what the judge wanted her to learn from all this?

That judge hadn't wanted her to learn anything. He'd only wanted the fifteen minutes of fame he'd get by sentencing Hollywood's favorite bad girl. With a whole generation of celebrity princesses making headlines with their less-than-legal antics, he'd decided to make an example of one of them. Rachel was the unlucky one to draw the short straw.

But even as the thought sped through her mind, she admitted how childish it sounded, which only frustrated her more.

Stepping quickly across the grounds toward her suite, she admitted she wasn't as angry as she was embarrassed. She'd made a bold pass at a man who ended up telling her off as if she were a schoolgirl. And despite the humiliation, what ultimately pushed her to tears was the acceptance that much of what he'd said was true. She *was* spoiled and afraid. She'd never worked a day in her life, and the things she had tried had been colossal failures.

What if she failed at this, too?

No one could have faulted her for not being able

to act. Her mother's career was a hard one to follow. Everyone in Hollywood knew that. Her clothing line bombed, her signature perfume was met with tepid sales. She'd tried to boost the ratings on her reality TV show by doing the spread for *Hush*. All she'd ended up with was a cancelled first season and semi-naked pictures all over the world.

Now, she was faced with the simplest task of all. Cleaning up a messy room. Children in grade school do it. What kind of a hit would it slap to her ego if she failed at that, too?

Rounding the back of the building, she made her way through her private terrace and toward the French doors that opened to the living room of her suite, her chin quivering and her eyes blurry with tears. Oh, God, she was a mess. She prayed that no one with a camera was near.

Holding herself together for the last few steps, she closed the terrace gate behind her, bursting into sobs the moment she stepped inside and closed the door to her suite.

Stefan instantly came running. "Rachel, what happened?"

Collapsing on the couch, she buried her face in her hands and cried, too upset for words, and not knowing where she would start if she had them.

Her angry heart wanted to spew out all kinds of horrible things about Marc and this resort. She wanted to tell Stefan that Marc was mean and cruel, that he'd humiliated her. She wanted to get on the phone to her father, ask him to send a car to take her out of here.

But her head only heard the bratty child in all those words, the one she'd grown tired of before she'd even shown up at this resort. While Marc might have been cruel, he'd told it like it was, and the truth hurt. It didn't mean that she'd forgive him, but it did mean she had no basis to cry foul.

Taking a seat next to her, Stefan put his arm around her shoulder and whispered calming words. She didn't need to tell him what Marc had said to know how he would react. Stefan would gasp and fume and tell her Marc had no right. He'd waltz back to Marc's office and tell him off. And in the end, he would perpetuate the same sense of entitlement that got her here in the first place.

Shaking off his questions, she asked for a tissue and a glass of water. Her throat hurt and her eyes stung, but somewhere in it all, answers began to form.

This was a situation she needed to handle herself. Calling for her father or sending Stefan on a rampage would only prove every mean word that Marc had uttered. Instead, what she needed to do was shove them all back in his face.

And Rachel knew there was only one way to do that.

"There now," Stefan said, handing her a glass of water and two tissues. "Drink this and tell me what's got you so upset."

She set the water aside and used the tissue to dab her eyes. "It's not important," she said.

"Don't be silly. If it's got you in tears, it's important."

Rising from the couch, she wrapped her arms around her chest, feeling chilly and unsure but in desperate need of proving a point, as much to Marc as to herself. Over the past few years, she'd lost everything, including her pride. Now, the only thing she had left was her stubborn will to fight, which was exactly what she'd do.

She wasn't going to leave this place on her first day. It would only feed more fodder to the tabloids that were anxious for her to fail all over again. And she wasn't going to leave this place giving Marc the satisfaction of knowing that he'd stood his ground and won. She needed to prove him wrong, prove *all of them* wrong.

For the first time in her life, Rachel was going to win, if only in this battle between her and the man who infuriated and excited her all at once. And if she failed at this, too, at least she'd know she'd gone down swinging.

Stefan picked up her glass and shoved it toward her. "Come on. Drink this. Tell me what happened and we'll fix it together."

"There's nothing for you to fix," she finally said. "This is something I need to handle on my own."

Then she turned and eyed Stefan with all the seriousness she could muster. "I want you to take your planner and all your things and go home."

4

"OH, MY, ARE YOU...?"

Brett looked up from a stack of achingly boring résumés to find a tanned and beautiful blonde standing over him, one hand on her hip and the other pointing a finger.

"You are!" she gushed. Her sexy smile widened. "Brett Strauss, right?"

His interest piqued. Fashion-model tall, she had long, wavy hair, full, pink lips and a nice curvy figure that was sweet on the eyes. Slim legs teased out of a knee-length skirt, but there was nothing conservative about the pale green T-shirt she wore with it. Two very shapely breasts poured over the low-cut neckline, taking the simple ensemble from average to extremely interesting in one low scoop.

"That's me." He brushed the résumés aside, curious to know where he might have met her. While his travels had brought him in contact with countless women, he couldn't imagine forgetting this one. She was the stuff memories were made of.

She took a seat at his table, uninvited but welcome nonetheless. Brett had spent the past hour in the café slamming Red Bulls trying to conjure up interest in the pile of paperwork in front of him. Needing to fill an opening in the pro shop, he'd left it to their office manager to place an ad in the paper, forgetting to tell the woman he wasn't exactly a résumé kind of guy. He'd preferred that the applicants simply stop by, figuring he'd know a good candidate when he saw one. Instead, he was stuck with a pile of dribble that told him practically nothing.

Shoving the whole task aside for a lush and curvy blonde? No brainer.

"I saw you down in Delray," she explained. "It must have been three—no, four years ago."

He grinned. "You follow tennis."

She gave him a sultry smile that sped straight to his privates. "I follow *you*. I mean, I did until you disappeared from the circuit. You played an amazing match down there against Todd Florence. That last set went six-four, didn't it?"

"Six-three, but who's counting?"

Setting her brown leather clutch on his stack of papers, she crossed her legs and got comfortable. "I thought you were going to make it all the way that year, but then you lost in the semifinals and *poof*, you were gone. What happened?"

He pointed to his shoulder. "Torn rotator."

She gasped. "Bad?"

"Threw me into early retirement."

She made a poor-baby face as if she might tear his shirt off and try to kiss it better. He wouldn't mind at all if she tried.

"I didn't catch your name," he said.

"Sorry." She held out a hand. "Margaret O'Dell, Brett Strauss Fan Extraordinaire."

He accepted it with a grin he hoped didn't look too eager. He hadn't had one of those in years. When his tennis career ended on the brink of mainstream success, he'd been shocked by how quickly the general public forgot him. Ranked a few points higher, he might have landed a job in broadcasting, but his shoulder blew a couple years too soon. In the end, his life had worked out well, though. Marc had come up with the idea to partner in this resort, and with Brett's career suddenly up for grabs, starting up a golf and tennis resort seemed to be the perfect answer.

But he sure did miss the groupies.

"Margaret, nice to meet you."

Dimitri, his server, approached the table. "Can I get you something here?"

Margaret touched a hand to her chest and glanced around the table. "Oh, I didn't mean to interrupt. You're obviously in the middle of something—"

"In the middle of something boring," Brett said. "How about a drink or a bite to eat?"

"I'll, um…how about a glass of white wine." She glanced down at her watch. "It's not too early for a drink, is it?"

"Not too early at all." He gestured to Dimitri. "A glass of wine and I'll take a beer." The man shuffled off and he turned back to Margaret. "So what brings you to the resort?"

"A long overdue vacation."

He glanced at her wedding finger. Bare. "Are you here with a friend?"

"Just me, myself and I." She glanced at *his* wedding finger. "How about you? Are you here for business or pleasure?"

"I own the place."

He loved saying that, especially when it got him the impressed look on a sexy woman's face, much like the one he was getting now.

"So this is what you've been doing since retirement." Their drinks arrived and she held up her wine for a toast. "Here's to life after tennis."

He tapped her glass with his beer, wondering if that life after tennis would include a few fun-filled days with a hot and all-alone blonde.

"Maybe you could show me around the place." She flicked a brow. "I'd love to know where the excitement is out here in the desert."

Oh, he could definitely point her to the excitement. It was a short drive to his condo.

He watched as she brought the rim of her glass to those plump, luscious lips and took a dainty sip of her wine, all the while trying to keep the glee from flashing on his face like a bright neon sign. When was the last time a beautiful single woman showed up at the resort looking for some fun? Okay, so maybe it had only been a few weeks, but that didn't temper his joy. Unlike his brother, who seemed to be waiting for that one special someone to come along, Brett liked his women in fast and frequent multipacks. And if that shapely body or those dark steamy eyes were any indication, he'd just found the perfect candidate for his flavor of the month.

They spent the next half hour getting to know each other. She told him she was in advertising and on the brink of job burnout, here for as many weeks as it took to dig up the will to go back—which she admitted might be never. She'd mentioned a couple accounts she'd worked on, companies he'd never heard of, but that didn't seem to bother either of them. In the course of having their drinks, it became pretty evident their interest in each other wasn't at all work-related.

He was about to suggest plans for a date when his cell phone rang. It was Rachel, the other beautiful and single woman to grace his resort this week. Though, unlike Margaret, Rachel's situation put her strictly off-limits for anything more than casual friendship. While Brett wasn't the most discriminating man, he knew better than to dip a toe into the sticky quagmire that was Rachel and her arrangement with the resort. But she was still fun to look at, nonetheless.

Man, he loved his job.

"Excuse me for a moment." He flipped open the phone. "Rachel?"

"Are you busy?" Rachel asked.

He glanced at Margaret. "For a while, why?"

MARGARET WORKED HARD to contain herself while she listened to Brett's half of his conversation. Could it be so perfect that the Rachel on the other end was Rachel Winston? If so, this was even better than she expected.

She took a sip of her wine to stifle a wide grin. God, men were easy. After weeks of investigation, she'd decided that the best way to gain the inside scoop on Rachel's sentence was to cozy up to the resort's notorious playboy co-owner. Though the idea offered no guarantees, she figured it was worth a try. Never in her dreams did she expect it would go this smoothly. Apparently, when her friend over at *Tennis World* magazine had said to hit him with cleavage, she hadn't been kidding.

Thank you, low-cut T-shirt.

She watched as Brett chatted, wondering how much

information she'd be able to pull from the man over the next few weeks. She'd promised her editor at the *National Star* plenty of reportable dirt if he'd only foot the bill for the room and not ask questions. The man was well aware that hungry new reporters would do anything for a story, and when she'd given him her high-level plan, he'd smiled knowing exactly what that *anything* would include.

Not that hopping into bed with Brett Strauss could be considered a hardship. The man was drop-dead gorgeous with his spiky blond hair and bone-melting dimples, not to mention that body. Obviously, retirement hadn't kept him from the gym. He looked as buff in person as he did in those years-old Internet photos she'd drummed up.

Nope, getting naked with this man definitely wouldn't be a problem, as long as his lips were as loose as the fly on his jeans. Margaret needed to be Brett's new confidante, and as long as she could keep him talking, the rest would be a picnic.

"Sorry for the interruption," he said, snapping the phone shut.

She flashed a sexy, woe-is-me pout. "You have a girlfriend."

"Rachel? No, she's just a friend. Purely platonic." He gave her an appreciative glance. "I was actually wondering if you'd like to have dinner with me."

"I'd love to. How about tonight?"

He checked his watch. "I've got some things to take care of, but I should be done around six. How does that sound?"

She smiled and rose from the table, holding out a

hand to the man who was about to help burst her career wide-open.

"It sounds like this trip will be everything I'd hoped."

RACHEL OPENED THE DOOR of her suite, relieved to find it was Brett who had knocked and not another reporter posing as room service. Having Stefan around to run interference was just another on the long list of things she'd somehow taken for granted, and it wasn't the first time today that she'd second-guessed her decision to send him home.

Brett walked through the door. "Hey, what's up?"

"Tell me you know something about computers," she begged.

He shrugged. "I know a little, I guess. What do you need?"

She stepped over to the desk Stefan had set up and picked up the instructions he'd left. "I can't get into this thing. It's password protected, but the stupid password doesn't work. Any idea how to get around that?"

He balked. "For that you'd need a hacker." He glanced around the room. "What about Stefan? Has he tried?"

"He's gone back to L.A."

"When's he coming back?"

"He's not."

He stared at her quizzically.

"I really don't need him while I'm here."

She'd tried to throw out the remark casually, as if it was totally normal for her to spend four weeks working as a maid in a resort a hundred miles from home without Stefan by her side. Apparently, Brett knew her better than she'd realized.

"Stefan's *gone?*"

"I'm a grown woman. I don't need a babysitter."

The argument hadn't worked on her parents ten years ago, but she hoped it worked on Brett now. If for no other reason than to help convince herself, as well, because right now she was feeling about as self-sufficient as a three-year-old.

"I just need help getting into my computer." She held out the note Stefan had stuck to the screen then took a seat at the desk. "Here's the password he left me, but it doesn't work." Clicking the cursor into the space provided, she typed out Birgit42. "See? Birgit42. It's his mother's name and the year she was born, but it's not working."

"It's Brigit42," he said, reading from the note. "You typed Birgit."

She snapped the note from his hand. Had it really been something so silly? A hot flush sped up her cheeks.

"I hate that it doesn't let me see what I typed. I just get those dumb dots."

Frustrated from spending the past half hour trying to get into her own computer, she pushed up from the desk and let Brett type it in. It worked perfectly.

"I understand what you mean about the password thing," he said in an attempt to shrug off her stupidity. "That's hung me up a couple times myself."

Needing to hide the flush on her cheeks, she crossed the room to the bar and pulled a bottle of water from the refrigerator. What was wrong with her? It had been a simple mistake, certainly not worthy of the gut-wrenching panic that had come over her the second the password hadn't worked. Too quickly, she'd let it fluster her, fearing that if she couldn't handle her first task without Stefan, she'd never make it an entire month.

Come down from your ivory tower and see how real people live.

Marc's angry words fled back to her, and she twisted the lid off her water and took a long drink. She had to stop this familiar chill of inadequacy from forming around her. It slipped in too easily, always cloaking her like a shadow and pushing her back to those few places where she felt smart and safe. She was stronger than that. All she needed to do was believe it.

"You need help with anything else?" Brett asked.

"No. Thanks." She took a deep breath to settle her nerves. "I just panicked when I couldn't get in. I really didn't want to have to call Stefan two hours after I'd sent him home. But I've got appointments I need to cancel. Marty was planning to drive up here tomorrow and I need to stop him before he leaves."

Brett rose from the desk. "Your chef? I already told you we'd be happy to accommodate him."

"I don't need him, or my Tuesday spa day, or any special hypoallergenic cleaning products. I'm perfectly capable of spending four weeks here on my own."

There. She said it again. And the more she repeated it, the easier it would be to buy it.

"I don't understand. Why the sudden—" Brett's eyes narrowed and he crossed his arms over his chest. "You met with Marc this morning."

She squared her shoulders. "You two spoke?"

"No, but I'm putting two and two together. Sending Stefan home, canceling your chef—listen, Rachel, I know how Marc can be. If he said anything to offend you, I'll go straighten him out right now."

She'd love for Brett to go straighten him out. A crowbar would be her tool of choice. But despite the bitter slap she'd taken to her pride, she couldn't deny that Marc had said a few things that stuck. What she didn't know was whether her reaction to it was the right thing to do, or if it was just another classic impulsive move destined to swing back and slap her in the face.

She wished she were thinking clearly enough to tell, but she was still flustered over the events of the day.

And still reeling from the effects of that sizzling kiss.

She slugged back another large gulp of water, wishing she could get the taste of him off her lips. She flexed her hand, trying to shake off the feel of that hard body still tingling on the tips of her fingers. Her decisions would all be so much clearer if she weren't working through a fog of unprecedented attraction. And when it came to Marc, that fog was thick and prickly.

Never had a man so infuriated and intrigued her all at once, to the point where she didn't know if she was thinking through her head or her hormones. She wanted desperately to prove a point to the jerk, but when she set aside her insult, she knew that she also wanted him to like her, to look at her with the same desire and admiration she felt for him. It was the only way she could walk away from here with her pride intact. So despite her reservations, she'd started on this path and intended to see it through.

"I don't need you to do anything with Marc. The meeting went fine. He simply gave me a couple things to think about and I've decided to make some changes."

If you weren't so spoiled and afraid, you might actually get something out of this.

She downed the last of her drink, but the sweet taste of him still lingered along with the bitter flavor of his words. Damn him.

"If you're sure."

"You said I'd be working with someone named Anita. When does that start?"

"Whenever you'd like it to."

"Does she work tomorrow?"

"Yes, she works Monday through Friday, eight to five."

"Then I'll work Monday through Friday, eight to five."

"Rachel—"

"And I want to really work. I don't want to be handed a bunch of fluff jobs. I want a real job like you'd give anyone else."

"Now I *know* that's my brother talking. C'mon, Rachel, what happened in that meeting?"

"Nothing." If you don't count turning her body to liquid with one hot and hungry kiss then torching it with a scolding that hit every touchy nerve she'd ever harbored.

"It's not about Marc," she went on. "It's about me taking a four-week time-out from Stefan and all the people who mean well, but have made it their job to run my life. I want to try running it myself."

He moved to the bar and searched her face. And when he seemed satisfied, he nodded. "I can understand that."

"I just might need an occasional hand." She smiled sheepishly. "Like when I can't spell my own password."

"You've got it." He checked the time. "I've got a couple hours before my dinner date. How about I take you around the facilities? Anita and Jolie are still here. I can introduce you to them and let them know you'll be starting tomorrow. There are a dozen other people on the staff who will kill me if I don't eventually introduce you to them. And it will help you to know who the good ones are. So, how about it? Would you like the grand tour?"

For the first time since her meeting with Marc, she started to feel calm and grounded. Knowing Brett was around if she needed him helped a lot. And based on what he'd said, not to mention the welcoming greeting she'd received from the staff she'd met so far, she started to think she might really be able to do this.

She stepped back to the computer and sat down to bring up her address book. "Let me give Marty and Gwen a quick call, then you're on."

5

HE REALLY SHOULDN'T HAVE kissed her.

On Marc's list of regrettable moves, he'd have to place kissing Rachel Winston somewhere near the top. Probably just below the time he'd borrowed his dad's new Beemer without asking then stacked it three blocks from the house. Torturing himself with a sampling of Rachel's body then thinking he could go about his day had ended up nearly as stupid.

He stood on the terrace overlooking the fountain, while Paige, his event coordinator, went over the details of a wedding taking place that weekend. With a golf tournament running concurrently, he really should be paying attention. Instead, his mind kept going back to how good Rachel's lips had felt on his, how his heart had surged with the simple touch of her waist against his palms, the dizzying fragrance of her sweet perfume. What he'd give to crawl between the sheets with her naked body and see exactly how much steam they could produce over the course of one night. Or a week. Enough to power a freight train, he suspected, judging by the lasting effects of that one measly kiss.

But he wasn't supposed to be thinking about things

like that, not now, not ever. Paige was going over the
script for the wedding, and unless he wanted to spend
his Saturday serving cake for lack of staff, he needed to
start listening. Heck, maybe even take a note or two.

He glanced around the garden area trying to remember where he'd set his notepad when a terse huff sounded
from across the stone walkway.

"You haven't heard a word I've said."

Marc spun around to see Paige standing in the shade
of a lemon tree, a clipboard in her hand and an impatient
look on her face. He tugged at his collar. The weather
report had predicted mideighties today, but damned if
it didn't feel warmer.

"Is it hot out here?" He unbuttoned his shirtsleeves
and rolled them up.

"It's summer in the Coachella Valley. Look, if
you want to do this another time, I can rearrange my
schedule."

Paige had a no-nonsense style that he'd always re-
spected, though much of the staff considered her a bitch.
He'd figured that was their problem, until now, having that disapproving glare directed at him. While it
was entirely his own fault, he now understood how the
woman might be considered intimidating. She wasn't
the least bit amused, nor did she seem to care that he
was technically her boss.

"I'm sorry," he said. "You were talking about the
fountain."

She eyed him warily but went on. "The ceremony
will be short, probably no longer than twenty minutes.
That means I'll need someone from maintenance here
by three-thirty."

"Assign someone on your end to make sure that
happens. With the tournament going on, they're going

to have their hands full. Don't leave it up to Kyle to remember."

She flashed a sour smile. "I never do."

He rubbed the back of his neck and tried to recall the notes he'd made about the two events. They'd already gone over the kitchen staff and the need to bring in extra help for the servers. With the reception dinner starting only an hour after the post-tournament buffet, they would have their hands full. What else was there?

He glanced around again for his pad. He'd been making notes that morning while he waited for his meeting with Rachel.

Crap, what to do with Rachel. He really should track her down and apologize for the way he'd spoken to her. Yes, he'd meant every word of it. And yes, he wholeheartedly believed she'd needed to hear it. But it hadn't been his place to judge her, and he'd gone way over the line considering she was, in some respect, a pseudoguest at the resort. He still couldn't believe he'd popped off like that, and he'd been feeling ashamed ever since. The problem was, in order to apologize he'd need to go see her. And seeing her meant being near her. And it seemed every time he came near her, he took one look at that brain-scrambling body of hers and all his gentlemanly tendencies packed up and flew south for the winter.

Would it be cowardly to send her a handwritten note?

"I lost you again," Paige called from across the terrace. This time she wasn't waiting but making a beeline toward the door. "I've got the parents of the bride showing up in fifteen minutes. When I'm done, I'll write this all out and leave it on your desk."

"Paige, I'm sorry." He snapped back to attention but

it was already too late. She was reaching for the door to the reception room.

"Don't worry about it," she said. "I know you've got a lot going on with Rachel Winston showing up yesterday. I'll just type up the main details and we can regroup after you've looked them over." Then she pulled open the door and disappeared into the building.

Dammit, this was ridiculous. Not since he started dating had a woman ever put him in a lusty haze this thick. Most definitely, he'd never let one interfere with his goals or his business. He'd always been driven, focused on the central task of owning and operating a resort. And while several girlfriends had vied to put themselves ahead of that, he'd never let one push him to the point of distraction.

Until now.

He plopped down on one of the stone benches and took in the beauty of the valley and the mountains beyond. It was late June and the orange and lemon trees were just bearing their fruit, lending a fresh citrus overtone to the sweet roses surrounding them. He soaked it all in as a reminder of why he needed to keep his mind on task. This resort was everything he'd ever wanted for as far back as he could remember.

The hospitality business had seeped into his blood when he was a kid and it had never left him. Whenever people asked why he wanted to own a resort, his answer was always, "How come you don't?" This was a place where precious memories were made. People married here, won awards, celebrated achievements and bonded as a family. For whatever reason they came, this resort represented a special time in their lives, and Marc got the daily pleasure of being a part of that.

But along with that pleasure came the overwhelming

burden of making sure those moments weren't ruined. His guests put their faith in him and the staff not to let them down, and that was exactly what would happen if he went about his day with his mind on what was under Rachel's skirt.

He needed to get it together, sooner than later, so pushing up from the bench, he set off to go make that apology he owed Rachel. When that was done, he'd put Jolie in charge of her stay and start the process of seriously wiping his thoughts of her and her sinful body for the next four weeks.

He made it as far as the poolside café when he heard Rachel's voice and the sound of Brett's laughter. Stepping to the gated entrance, he found them standing near the bar chatting with Miguel, the bartender.

Rachel was still wearing the sexy dress that had driven him mad that morning, and when he caught a good glimpse, he realized that even his memory had diminished how stunning she was.

His feet rooted in place as he watched the three converse. Brett cracked a joke and she laughed and placed a hand on his shoulder, sending a biting wave of envy down the back of Marc's spine. This wasn't right, this feeling of possession. Nor was the longing in his gut that gripped his jaw and muted his speech. She was just a woman, a hot, beautiful woman, of which there were dozens in a place like this. So why was he letting this one get so far under his skin?

Whatever the reason, the need and lust and jealousy had to go. He cleared his throat and forced his legs to move forward. The gesture caught their attention, and when Rachel turned and saw him, the easy smile slid from her face. She stiffened, and while she wasn't exactly glaring at him with hatred, he definitely got the impression that the wet blanket had arrived.

It grated on him more than it should have, throwing hurt into the stew of mixed emotions that was already burning his insides.

"How's everything going?" he asked.

"Great." Brett smiled, oblivious to the tension surrounding him. "I've been showing Rachel around, introducing her to some of the staff."

Miguel flashed a wide grateful grin.

"We caught up with Jolie and Anita just now," Brett added. "Rachel's starting in housekeeping tomorrow morning."

Marc blinked. "Tomorrow's Tuesday. I thought that was your spa day." Somehow, he managed to make the remark without any added twinge of sarcasm.

"Rachel's—" Brett started, but she quickly cut in.

"I've rearranged my plans." She jutted that sweet, dimpled chin then turned back to Brett and smiled. "Speaking of which, we should move on. I've got a number of things to take care of this evening, and I'd like to turn in early so I'm fresh for tomorrow."

She took Miguel's hand and offered sweetly, "It was a pleasure to meet you."

The man lapped it up. "You know where to find me." Then he pointed a finger. "And don't forget, jalapeño is the new pomegranate. You stop by and I'll make you one of my famous hot pepper martinis."

She chuckled. "It's a date." Then without so much as a glance Marc's way, she gestured to Brett. "Walk me back?"

"Actually," Marc said. "I was hoping I could have a word with Rachel."

She raised a brow. "I think I've had enough of your words for one day."

He should have known she wouldn't make this easy, but knowing he deserved it, he pressed on. "I owe you a couple more, including an apology."

She sized him up, clearly surprised. He could see those blue eyes calculating, and he thought she would concede to come with him. Instead, she squared her shoulders. "Apology accepted. Now, if you'll excuse me. I have a long day ahead of me tomorrow and I really need my rest." She took Brett's arm. "Shall we?"

"Rachel," Brett said, "maybe you two should clear the air."

"Oh, we cleared plenty of air this morning. I found it rather unsatisfying." She shot Marc a glance stuffed with innuendo. "Now, if you don't mind, I really need to move on."

Unsatisfying?

Marc balled his fists at his sides to keep from reaching out and grabbing her. Unfortunately, if he caught hold, he wasn't sure if he'd end up shaking her senseless or kissing her silly. The woman was as exasperating as she was sexy, which made it all the more ludicrous that through all that spit and fire he only wanted her more.

"Rachel—" Brett started, but Marc held up a hand.

"That's quite all right. Our guest is tired. I don't want to keep her."

Had that come across as juvenile as he feared? The last thing he needed was to come off like a rejected lover. Mostly because that was exactly how he felt. But he couldn't afford a public scene, and as he considered the situation, he concluded that he was probably better off if she hated him. At least it would keep her at a distance.

Brett glanced between the two, then gave up. "Fine, let's go."

And as he and Rachel walked off, Miguel whistled soft and slow. "Wow, ice. What did *you* do?"

Marc watched those erotic hips sway as she disappeared through the gate and down the path. "Someday, I'll tell you all about it over one of those martinis."

"I'll hold you to it, *mi amigo*."

"MAKING BEDS IS SURE easier with two people." Anita snapped the starched white sheet and let it float down over the bed. "I'm going to be spoiled by the time you're gone."

Rachel appreciated the kind words even though she had a hard time believing them. "I think I've been more of a hazard than a help these past three days." She grabbed her end of the sheet and pulled it taut.

Anita smiled. "You're doing fine. I think it's better you've never cleaned before. You aren't bringing along a lot of bad habits, you know?"

"You're sweet," Rachel said, and she meant it.

Anita Cooper was a plump woman with a pretty face, a turned-up nose and glowing skin that Rachel would die for. And she was just about the nicest person Rachel had met in ages.

After three days together on the job, Rachel had learned that when it came to Anita, what you saw was what you got. There was nothing fake or presumptuous about her, nor was she a giddy fan girl. And after growing up in the plastic world of L.A., Rachel found it extremely refreshing.

This was exactly the kind of life she'd imagined when daydreaming about moving abroad—doing normal things with normal people who weren't looking for something to gain other than simple friendship. She caught glimpses of that kind of life when she and Anita took their daily breaks in the employee room with the other housekeeping staff. Sure, on her first day people were reserved, not knowing what to make of her or how to act around her. But by this morning's break, they'd all resumed what Rachel assumed was their normal banter, and she was envious of the ease with which they conversed. The coworkers talked about everything, sharing intimate details of their lives regardless of who came and went from the room. They laughed and consoled, traded secrets and insights in a way Rachel had abandoned years ago.

Too many times in her past, she'd talked like that with friends only to find her words twisted and plastered over the tabloids the following week. She'd had to learn the hard way not to open up to casual friendships, even though it went against her outgoing nature. And when she watched these men and women sharing themselves so easily, she yearned to do the same.

So often, she'd wanted to disappear from the spotlight, and on more than one occasion, she'd gone off to try life in some anonymous locale. But within a matter of weeks, boredom snuck in, and with no real skills or lasting hobbies, she'd gone back to L.A. defeated for lack of something meaningful to do. Watching them all together left her tempted to try it again.

"I don't think I'll win any Best Housekeeping awards," Rachel said. "But I have to admit, there's something calming about the work."

Anita tossed her two pillows and cases. "It's funny you say that, because it's exactly the way I feel about the job." She held a pillow under her chin while she slipped the clean white case over it. "I like that I don't have any bosses hovering over me. I get to work on my own in the quiet of the empty rooms. And I find that busy fingers open up my creative side and help me think."

Rachel mirrored Anita's movements, covering one pillow then closing up the end like the woman had shown her. "Your creative side?"

"I write books in my spare time."

"Really?"

"Yeah. My daughter Kelsey and I are trying to get some young adult fiction published. We haven't sold anything yet, but the novel we're working on now is our best yet. I have high hopes for it. Anyway, I spend most of my time here at work keeping my hands busy while I mentally plot and plan out scenes." She pulled a small spiral pad from her smock pocket. "I take notes so I don't forget the good stuff. And after dinner, Kelsey and I spend our evenings working on it."

She tucked the notepad back in her pocket and shrugged. "We may never publish anything together. Kelsey's the one with the real talent. But in the meantime, I'm enjoying spending the time with her. Most teenagers don't want to hang with their parents, so I'm lucky we have the writing to keep us close."

"That's so cool."

They continued putting fresh linens on the bed, Rachel tucking the corners the way Anita had shown her. Over the past few days, she'd heard dozens of stories like Anita's as the two passed the time by chatting about all the people who worked at the resort. She was quickly putting real lives behind the faces of the staff, and it took her back to the accident that had put her here.

She insisted on calling it an accident because she'd never intentionally hurt someone, but that didn't excuse her actions.

She'd been enjoying a long weekend at a resort in San Diego when her agent had called with what was another installment in a long string of disappointing news. They'd ended up getting into a terrible fight, and when her agent hung up on her, Rachel had been so furious she'd snapped her cell phone shut and flung it across the room. She hadn't even seen the maid stepping from the bathroom, and the phone had hit the woman square on the temple, cutting open her head and leaving her with a mild concussion, according to the doctor's reports.

And while it was a genuine accident, it was Rachel's actions after the fact that had created all her problems. Instead of apologizing immediately and tending to the woman, she'd blamed her for sneaking into the room and accused her of eavesdropping. She'd let the incident further her tirade, and she'd treated the woman as if she were no more valuable than the chair in the corner.

If Rachel hadn't been ashamed enough before, she was even more so now. As she worked to put a fresh coverlet on the down comforter, she considered something like that happening to Anita, and it nearly brought tears of shame to her eyes. She'd acted horribly, and for the first time since it happened, she began to understand why the judge might have sentenced her so harshly.

"Done," Anita said. She pointed to the dark wood dresser and table in the room. "Why don't you start dusting while I go tackle the bathroom?"

"Actually, how about if *I* do the bathroom and *you* dust?"

Anita waved her off. "Don't worry about it. I don't mind."

"Really, I don't want special treatment. Let me do the bathroom."

"Hon, this room is a checkout. We've got to scrub

the whole thing down. You do the next one where we just straighten up."

"I'm serious. You've already shown me what to do." She made her way to the cart in the hall and pulled on a pair of gloves. "Let me do it."

"Well, you are a stubborn one, aren't you?"

Rachel smiled. "Yes, actually, I am."

Anita handed her the proper cleaning products, reminding her which one to use on the tile and which one on the mirrors, then Rachel sauntered off. Though she'd spent the past several weeks hating the judge who'd sentenced her and feeling nothing but sorry for herself, she had to admit this experience was affecting her in ways she hadn't expected.

She thought back to the day she'd arrived here. She'd been at her lowest and had hoped something positive might come out of the stay. At the time she'd been thinking meditation, relaxation and reflection, but in this turn of events, she was beginning to find her sense of renewal through the people she was meeting and this work they shared. It was a pathetic statement to her existence that the simple task of learning how to make a bed gave her a sense of gratification. These were things other people took for granted—dreaded, even. But to Rachel it felt like…independence.

"We're out of furniture polish," Anita said. "I've got to go get more, but I'll be right back."

"No problem."

Rachel stepped into the bathroom and looked around, pleased to see it wasn't even very dirty—certainly not the mess like she'd seen in some of the other rooms. They'd already pulled all the towels and dropped them in the hamper. She'd cleared the vanity of all the complimentary products and emptied the wastebaskets. With all the clutter gone, the rest of the job seemed easier to tackle.

She considered the best place to start and decided to start with the biggest job first, which was the oversize walk-in shower. The enclosure was spacious enough for two, encased with a frameless glass door, floor-to-ceiling marble and featured a wide chrome showerhead that hung from the ceiling. It was much like the shower she had at home, large and luxurious. And today she'd find out exactly what it took to clean it. So setting the products on the marble vanity, she took the scrub sponge and spray cleaner and stepped inside.

She did as Anita had shown her, starting by spraying down all the walls then letting the cleaner soak in a bit before wiping it down with the sponge. She hummed as she worked, busily scrubbing the walls in circles just like Anita had shown her, when the click of the shower door opening caught her attention. She assumed it was Anita, but before she could turn around, she heard the whir of the pipes just before the heavy spray began to rain down upon her.

She yelped and moved to grab the valve, confused and shocked, and in her alarm she turned the lever the wrong way sending the steady stream into a raging storm.

Jumping and screeching, she finally managed to shut it off, but not before she was blinded from the sting of the chemicals and wholly drenched to the core. She shook her head to get the wet strings of hair out of her face, unable to touch her eyes with the harsh chemicals on her gloves.

What the hell had happened? And if Anita had accidentally turned on the faucet, why wasn't she helping right now? She started to wipe her eyes with her forearms just as she heard the familiar snapping of a camera.

"Hey!" she called out. She swiped her arm over her face and blinked her eyes open to see a man she didn't recognize, holding an expensive SLR camera and snapping off shots.

"Hey! What the hell—" she started, then like a blur Anita came rushing through the door, a towel in her hand and fury in her eyes.

She started screaming expletives as she pushed and shoved at the photographer, slapping the towel over his head and trying to grab for the camera in his hand.

"You get the hell out of here!" she screamed. "Get out! Get out!" She had him by the scruff of his collar and he choked and stumbled back, the camera slamming against the doorjamb as he fought to maintain his balance.

"Hey, bitch!" he cried.

It only infuriated her more, and by the time the two stumbled out of the doorway the man was ducking and holding his arms up in defense.

"I'm going, you crazy bitch!"

"Crazy bitch? I'll have you thrown out of here!"

Then the scuffle faded out of the room and down the hall, leaving Rachel standing in the shower, cold, soaked and shaken. Her hands were trembling and she pulled off her gloves and moved to rinse them in the sink. It was only when she caught sight of her horrid reflection in the mirror that she realized what had happened. The ghostly face staring back at her would be a tabloid cover next week, another item on her long list of embarrassing moments for the grocery store checkout stands.

And as she stood pondering what ridiculous caption they'd splash over her picture, she wondered whether it was time to laugh or cry.

6

"HAPPY?"

Brett tossed a magazine on Marc's desk then stood there angrily awaiting a reaction. Not accustomed to seeing his brother mad, Marc glanced down, curious to know what could set him off.

All Washed Up, read the headline in bold yellow letters sprawled across an image he barely recognized as Rachel. She was standing in a shower—one of theirs, he realized—the gray uniform smock hanging oddly off one shoulder. Her hair was a mess, her hands covered in soapy rubber gloves, and the expression on her face was one of shock and mortification.

To say the photo was unflattering would be like calling Mt. Everest a short hill, and as he studied it, a dozen questions began running through his head.

"This is your fault," Brett snapped.

Marc blinked. "*My* fault?"

"I had this all worked out. Everything would have been fine if you'd just let me handle it."

"What did *I* do?"

"That's what I'd like to know, but Rachel won't talk about it. Whatever happened between you two in that meeting last week, you did something to set her off. Probably one of those classic, self-righteous lectures you're so good at. I don't know because she's not saying. But what I *do* know is she came out of it intent on proving something." He stepped from the desk and began pacing the spacious office. "You know she sent Stefan home."

Marc shook his head.

"Oh, yeah," Brett went on. "She cancelled all her appointments and told her friends to stay in L.A. Then she showed up for work and insisted she and Anita share everything evenly."

"What does that have to do with this picture?"

"She gave you exactly what you wanted. No special treatment, just like you've been harping on since the day she set foot here."

"I only want what the judge ordered."

"And that's what you got. You wanted her to be treated like any other regular person, except you forgot one thing." He stopped and placed his palms on Marc's desk. "Rachel Winston isn't a regular person. Regular people don't have photographers following them around looking for opportunities to humiliate them and plaster degrading photos of them all over the newsstands." He pushed up and crossed his arms over his chest. "Poor Anita is devastated. She thinks it's her fault for leaving Rachel alone without making sure the door was shut. I already straightened that out by assuring her there's only one person responsible for this."

"That's ridiculous." He took the tabloid in his hand and studied the photo. "I don't see how you can blame this on me."

"Do you know how pissed off Richard Winston's going to be when he sees this? We'd promised to keep the press away from her. And if you'd let me handle it, Rachel wouldn't have been doing anything that could humiliate her even if the press had gotten through." Brett paced over to the large window then turned and pointed a finger. "If he calls looking for an explanation, I'm patching him straight over to you."

Marc opened his mouth to defend himself when a tall blonde appeared at the open doorway. She poked her head in and smiled when she saw Brett. "Oh, there you are. They said you might be here." She glanced alternately between the two men. "Am I interrupting something?"

Brett checked his watch. "Oh, hell, I lost track of time."

The woman stepped into the office and held out a hand to Marc. "Hi, I'm Margaret."

Annoyed and confused, Marc accepted it, though his only response was to glare at his brother.

"You two are obviously dealing with a problem," Margaret said, turning to Brett. "If you want to cancel, we can go out another time."

"No, I'm not cancelling anything." Brett stepped to her side. "I'm done here, anyway." He pointed to the tabloid. "Someone needs to go talk to her and since it's your mess, I vote you deal with it."

"I—" Marc started.

"I'm not playing mediator between you two. You wanted to run this show, now you can fix it."

Then Brett turned and led the woman out the door.

"What was that all about?" he heard her ask as they stepped down the hall. Marc had to admit he had the same question.

Throughout their lives, he could count on one hand the times he'd seen Brett this angry. It left him flustered and still not fully computing what had happened. It was only when he returned to the photo and started reading the article that the shock faded and reality began to sink in.

Obviously, a reporter had gotten through and found Rachel in this compromising position. And obviously, Brett concluded it was Marc's fault even though he'd made it clear Rachel wasn't to be left alone at any time while she was working. And while his first reaction was to point the finger at Jolie and Anita, one or two of Brett's points snuck into his conscience and kept him from picking up the phone.

He stared at the photo and bit back a curse. She looked wet. How the hell had she managed to drench herself while fully clothed in a walk-in shower? He scanned over the article looking for more information when a light rap on the door caught his attention.

"Oh, so you've seen it," Jolie said, stepping into the room. She had guilt written all over her face, which was far more logical than the raking he'd just received from Brett. Marc had left Jolie in charge of Rachel. She was the one who had the explaining to do.

"When did this happen?" he asked.

"Last Thursday. I would have reported it, but Rachel kept insisting it was nothing to worry about."

A familiar annoyance came over him. "Since when does Rachel Winston call the shots?"

Jolie opened her mouth to reply then shut it when she realized she had none. Instead, she stepped into the office and took a seat at his desk.

"I'm sorry," she said. "You're right that I should have told you. It's just that Rachel asked us not to involve you, and, well…" She smiled apprehensively. "Rumor's going around that you two don't exactly get along. We didn't want to cause more trouble. She's been so kind to all the staff."

He stared at his head of housekeeping, the woman who had been running the department like a well-oiled machine since before he took over the resort three years ago. The woman he'd trusted wholeheartedly and thought he'd had a good rapport with.

The woman who, when given the choice between coming to him and covering for Rachel, quickly shoved that three-year relationship aside in favor of the celebrity.

"Even this afternoon when one of the guys brought the tabloid in," she went on, "her first concern was to make sure none of us took the blame for it."

"What a saint," he said flatly.

Anger and betrayal crept in to color his reaction, but when he forced himself to think clearly, he knew he had a part in this. After all, he was the one who had holed himself up in his office for a week trying to pretend Rachel wasn't under his roof. He was the one who'd set himself up as her adversary when his primary job here was to assure the smooth operation of the resort.

And when he let the nagging voice in his head speak clearly, Brett's words slipped in and blew away any final argument he might have had.

It was true. He hadn't considered Rachel's situation when he'd laid down his expectations. He'd made biased assumptions about her without understanding everything wasn't exactly black and white. And worse, he'd let his overwhelming desire for her body stop him from doing his job.

He leaned back in his chair and rubbed his hands over his face. "Do me a favor," he asked. "From now on, keep me in the loop on everything significant that goes on with Rachel."

"Absolutely. I'm sorry for not doing so earlier. This is a new situation for me and I—"

"It's a new situation for all of us. You aren't the only one who's made mistakes. Let's learn from it and move on."

She rose from her seat. "Of course. I'll go let Rachel know we've spoken."

"Let me," Marc said.

"You want to talk to Rachel yourself?"

No. No, he didn't. He'd spent a week working hard to keep his mind off her and his nose to the grindstone. Tracking her down and having a heart-to-heart wouldn't help. But this silliness had gone on long enough, and obviously, distance wasn't keeping either of them out of trouble. It was time they cleared the air and made a genuine effort to come to a truce.

And he needed to do it all without either killing or kissing her.

Taking the magazine in his hand, he rose from his desk. "This is something I need to handle."

RACHEL HAD JUST CHANGED into a comfortable pair of sweats when she heard the knock at the door. Assuming it was the room service she'd called for earlier, she opened it without hesitation, seeing only too late that it wasn't dinner but Marc Strauss.

Great. When would she learn to check before opening her door?

"You aren't room service," she said in an effort to buy time while she calculated the best way to brush him off. She'd had a long and humiliating day today. Ending it in the presence of this man wasn't tops on her list.

"No, they haven't demoted me yet," he said.

He grinned and she had to stifle a sigh. Oh, he was gorgeous when he smiled, something he didn't do nearly enough. It was probably a good thing, since when he did, those silvery blue eyes and pearly white teeth made her forget all kinds of things—namely that he was an ass and she wasn't supposed to want him.

"Well, if you aren't bringing me dinner, what do you want?"

He held up the magazine in his hand. "I'd like to talk."

"Huh, I would have pegged you as more of a *Newsweek* kinda guy."

He laughed jovially and she noticed for the first time that he had a dimple on his left cheek. She was a sucker for dimples, especially on a face like Marc's where that stubborn chin and straight brow brightened up with the playful touch. In fact, given the lethal effect of that stunning smile, she wondered why he didn't use it more often as the ace in the hole it was. There wasn't a woman on the planet that could turn down a request when delivered with that one-two punch.

"Yes, I suppose I am." His chuckle eased as his gaze slipped down to her breasts, the ones barely covered by her flimsy T-shirt and now shamelessly revealing the effects of that smile. And going by the glint in his eyes, he hadn't missed it.

He cleared his throat. "May I come in?"

Every part of her screamed *no,* but nonetheless, she found herself backing up and offering him access. *Damned one-two punch.*

He stepped into the room and held up the tabloid as she closed the door. "I wanted to apologize for this."

She looked down at the photo, sickness welling all

over again even though she'd thought she was over it. It would help if she weren't so attracted to the man holding it. When one of the maintenance engineers showed up with it today, she'd been embarrassed to say the least. But seeing Marc with the photo, when that pesky side of her still desperately wanted to impress him, added an extra dose of shame.

She reverted to her old defenses. "Forget about it. If I let the tabloids get to me I would have been in a straitjacket years ago." She waved a dismissive hand and moved to the bar where she'd left the glass of wine she'd started earlier. "Everyone around here is making a big deal out of nothing. It's just a stupid picture."

It was a good effort. One of her best, really. But when she turned and caught Marc's eye, she knew he hadn't bought it.

She never *had* been able to act.

"It's a big deal to us," he said. "We were supposed to protect you from the press and we let you down. I'm sorry for that."

Noting the word *we* in that sentence, she said, "I already made it clear to Jolie this wasn't Anita's fault. If you're here to place blame—"

He held up a hand. "This is *my* fault."

He took a long breath and tossed the magazine on the bar. "Look, Rachel, I haven't been fair to you since the day you set foot here. I've treated you badly then ignored my responsibilities where you're concerned. That's not anyone's fault but mine, and I need you to know how much I regret it."

Her cynical mood began to falter when she caught the sincerity in his eyes. He looked as if he really meant it, even though a voice in her head told her to hold her guard. This day had taken its toll and her defenses were down, the tabloid smear hurting more than she'd like to admit.

Over the week she'd been here, she'd genuinely grown fond of all the people she'd met. Though it seemed crazy, she even liked the work, loved being a part of a team. And then the photo hit the stands, reminding her and everyone else that while they'd welcomed her warmly, she'd never be the normal person she wanted to be. Reality had hit like a slap in the face, singling her out and separating her from the people she'd begun to consider friends.

Though she'd held her chin up, inside she hadn't taken it well. And now that the day was over, the energy it had taken left her drained and vulnerable, her hopeful side searching hard for a silver lining to cling to. Wouldn't a heartfelt apology and acceptance by Marc Strauss be just the ticket to salvage her day?

Marc casually leaned against the bar. "I've heard from a number of people that you've been very kind."

"People have been kind to me."

"And you've been working hard."

There was that smile again, packed with enough warmth and sincerity to unravel the last of the bitter grudge she'd been harboring for a week. Maybe this meeting would end her night on an upswing after all.

"I judged you unfairly." He pointed to the tabloid. "I've been no better than the people who believe crap like that."

She shrugged. "Don't judge them. Most of what they've printed about me is true."

She didn't know where the confession came from. They were on a roll here and she needed to leave as many balls in her court as possible. But seeing this sweet, friendly side of him tripped her up and made her feel as though they could be honest with each other.

"You didn't deserve this," he said. "And I'm sorry you got slammed with it. Brett and I, we promised your father we'd keep the press from your heels. I'm sure he'll be angry that we didn't do our job."

She blinked and stared. "What did you say?"

"I said, I'm expecting your father will be pretty irate when he sees this."

Her bubble of hope burst and all she could do was gape. Her father. Of course. How could she not have suspected the real motive behind all this candy-eyed remorse?

She huffed and shook her head. "I can't believe this. For a minute, you really had me going."

Tears threatened and her throat swelled, the culmination of the day bearing down on her and pushing her over the edge with this one final clap on the back. When would she learn?

"Excuse me?" he asked.

"You aren't sorry for any of this. You're only worried what my father will do. You're afraid he'll pull whatever deal he cut with you when he finds out you didn't keep up your end of the bargain."

God, how many times did she have to be used by men before she got it through her head? *I've treated you badly,* he'd said, delivered with such a solemn, regretful tone that she'd actually bought it.

"That's not true," he said, but she caught the tinge of fear and desperation in his voice. He probably hadn't figured her smart enough to catch on at all, let alone so quickly. "We don't have any deal with your father."

He stepped toward her and reached out a hand, but

she pushed away and rounded into the kitchen, putting the wide marble-topped bar between them. "Get out."

He had the gall to look astonished. "I'm serious. There's no deal with Richard. I'm here because of you."

"Don't insult my intelligence. I'm a lot more practiced at this game than you are."

"I'm not playing any games. Look, I'm sorry I gave you the wrong impression by mentioning Richard. I'm not here because of him. I'm trying to make peace with you."

"Why? To stay on good terms with my father?"

He held up his hands and spoke to the ceiling. "No. I just said this wasn't about your father. You're the most exasperating woman I've ever met!"

"Get out." She felt a tear roll down her cheek. *Brilliant.* "Just get out."

His expression was aghast as he started for the door, but before he took a second step, he stopped and balled his fists. "No. I'm not going anywhere." He turned and faced her. "You're going to listen to me and I'm not leaving until we've straightened this out. This idiocy is going to end."

She choked back a sob. "Oh, now I'm an idiot."

He took two strides and cornered her against the counter. "I didn't call you an idiot."

"No, but that's what you presumed when you set this deal up."

"I didn't set anything up, Brett did. And I told you there's no deal." A slow tide of redness began to creep from his collar up his neck. "And as far as presumptions, I had plenty. I thought you were spoiled, manipulative and lazy and I was wrong. I've owned up to that. I'm sorry. *Jeez, how many times do I have to say it?*"

She tried to squirm away but he only stepped closer. "Just go. I don't want you here."

"I'm not leaving us like this. You've got three more weeks here and I'm done tiptoeing around my own resort trying to avoid you. If we have to kill each other trying, we're going to find a way to get along."

She shoved against his chest, but it was like trying to topple Stonehenge. The man was hovering over her, cloaking her thoughts with the sound of his breath and that fresh springlike scent of turf and lemons and sweat. It was enough to drive her crazy.

"I'm sure there's a couple of knives around here somewhere."

The redness above his collar crept higher, nearly reaching his chin. "You're being ridiculous."

"Oh, first I'm an idiot, now I'm ridiculous."

He cursed under his breath. "I didn't say that."

"Get out." She shoved against his immovable form. "I'm done dealing with jerks like you. You come in and play all sweet and nice with that one-two-punch smile, but what's underneath is always the same. The only thing you really want from me—"

"Oh, for—" He grabbed her by the arms and covered her mouth with his, swallowing the rest of her sentence and swiping all thoughts from her head.

She had a passing whim to attempt a struggle, but lost it as soon as his hard, sexy body trapped her against the counter. The demanding clasp of his mouth, the possessive grip of his hands, the warm mass of his chest, it was all too good to turn away.

With the force of a brute, he parted his lips and shoved his tongue toward hers, and in all the defense of milquetoast, she opened her mouth to accept it. The taste of him caressed her senses, a hint of peppermint against that outdoorsy scent that seemed to seep from his pores. She stole a breath and drank it in, taking it like a stiff shot of whiskey to soothe the ache of her horrible day.

Talented hands went to work holding her close and seducing her will. The light brush of a thumb across her cheek, the tight squeeze of a hand against her waist, they slipped around her body in tender exploration, pouring heat through her veins where it circled around and pooled between her legs.

"That's better," he whispered before claiming her mouth again.

Through the mist her head kept screaming at her to slap him silly and push him off, but her body wouldn't obey, taking instead what it desperately needed. Not apologies. Not arguments and accusations. Only this commanding, sexy man holding her safe while those barraging lips plundered the hurt from her chest.

She sank against him, taking part in the sensual feast by sliding her hands under his suit jacket and up his back. A long, luxurious moan hummed up his throat, hitting a chord she felt all the way to the tips of her fingers. Her body grew heavy with desire, blood rushing to all her sensitive places and thrumming a beat in her ears. It was like stepping into a warm soothing spa, the heat of his embrace washing over her, smoothing the rough edges and draining away the stress of the day.

In his arms, she lost her grip on time and space. Memories of what they'd been fighting about slipped out of sight, taking a backseat to the glory of those lips and the steamy caress of those hands.

And just as she settled in to enjoy a long and sumptuous soak, a sharp rap at the door halted the momentum.

"Room service."

7

"DON'T ANSWER THAT," Rachel urged. She pulled Marc's mouth back to hers and resumed the only good thing that had happened to her all day. Longer, if she stopped to think about it.

"I have to. He won't go away," Marc said, though he stayed for another kiss nonetheless.

He caressed his hands up her waist, stealing her breath and pushing her blood from a low simmer into a hot sizzling boil. She couldn't remember a time when a simple kiss brought so much pleasure. It left her aching to find out what he could do if given full reign over her body.

She clutched her hands to his jacket and held on tight, fearing she might never find out if he stepped away and tended to the man at the door.

"Let it go. He'll leave," she urged, pressing her lips along his jaw to remind him how much fun they were having, just the two of them. She made her way along the rough peppering of his day-long beard, stopping when she reached his ear to whisper exactly what awaited him if he'd forget about the door and go to her bedroom instead.

His knees buckled and he groaned.

"Come on," she said. "I'm just beginning to like you. Don't ruin it all now."

He smiled and playfully kissed the tip of her nose. "I don't intend to, but he's not going away. Trust me. I'm the one who made the rules."

Marc left her and her body mourned, chilled from the loss of warmth. She gripped the counter for support while he straightened his tie and checked himself over.

"I'll get rid of him," he said, stepping quickly to the door where he flung it open and greeted the server with a bright smile.

"Mr. Strauss," the man said in obvious surprise.

"Armand, good to see you." Marc stood aside and let Armand roll the cart into the suite, and it was only then that Rachel realized she should stand straight and stop looking like a woman who'd just been ravaged by a dark and steely sex god.

"It seems as if I've come at a bad time," Marc said to Rachel, pasting a casual smile on his face. "I don't want to spoil your dinner. We can go over this paperwork another time, if you'd like."

He winked covertly and she tried hard not to swoon. If the man wasn't enticing enough when ravaging her body, he was even more delicious when lying through his teeth to protect their privacy.

"It's just a salad. It'll keep," she said. She pulled the covered plate from the cart and took it to the refrigerator. "I'd just as soon get it taken care of."

Marc pulled out his wallet and handed Armand a tip.

"Oh, that's not necessary, sir," Armand said, but Marc shoved it in his hand.

"Don't be silly. I'm keeping Ms. Winston from her dinner. The least I can do is cover her tip."

Armand nodded and smiled. "Thank you, sir."

And with quick strides, Marc led him out. Finally alone again, he leaned against the door and let out a long sigh. Rachel quickly rounded the bar toward him, intent on getting back to where they'd left off, but before she could, she caught him swallowing hard and running a shaky hand through his hair.

She stopped in her tracks and shook her head. "Oh, no, you're not going to do this to me."

He looked up. "Do what?"

"Don't even think about having second thoughts. I know that look on your face and I'll tell you right now, don't even try it. I'm not in the mood to hear what a mistake that kiss was and how wrong this is and all your regrets and apologies." She clenched her fists and braced herself for what was surely the next blow. Hope followed by rejection—the story of her life. Happiness torn apart by her situation, who her parents were, and all the stupid mistakes she'd made. She was sick of it, officially at the end of one long and knotted rope.

But instead of apologies, Marc reached out and pulled her into his arms.

He cupped her face in his hands. "This *is* wrong," he admitted.

She opened her mouth but he shut it with a quick kiss. "Given the circumstances," he went on, "this is a very bad idea and not entirely ethical." He kissed her again, longer, slower this time. And when he was done, he circled his arms around her. "Which only goes to show how badly I want you."

He slipped his hands down to her ass and squeezed, enveloping her once again in that warm heavenly embrace she'd wanted so badly. "What do you say we take this to the bedroom," he suggested, a sultry look of promise darkening those steel-gray eyes. Rachel didn't argue. If ever a day needed to end on a high note, this was it. And she couldn't think of a higher note than a big satisfying orgasm thanks to this hot and handsome stud.

"Let's go."

MARC PULLED OFF HIS TIE and unbuttoned his cuffs as he followed Rachel into the bedroom, his eyes never leaving the tight, sexy ass he'd just had his hands on.

He knew this would happen if he let himself get too close. He knew that dousing the fire of bitterness between them would only ignite a hotter one of desire. He also knew this could land both of them in a load of trouble if word of an affair leaked to the press, and worse, to the court.

A conflict of interest was obvious, threatening to negate all the work Rachel had done and put the resort under a mountain of speculation. But the tension between them had become too hot to ignore. The moment he'd placed his mouth on hers he knew he'd never be satisfied until he'd taken the whole package.

He'd had a fighting chance last week when the attraction was purely physical. But everything he'd heard and seen since then had opened a weakness in his heart, and when the need for her body met with the knowledge that there was a tender, considerate woman inside, his armor crumbled into dust.

The want was too severe, the hunger too great, and though he knew this could come back and bite him, right now he had to take what his body craved.

When she stepped inside the large master bedroom,

she pulled the white flimsy T-shirt over her head, revealing two luscious round breasts. The sight stopped his momentum and rooted him in place, unable to do anything but stare at that shapely form as she wiggled out of her sweats and stood naked before him.

There was the image, the one from *Hush* magazine that had haunted his dreams, and would probably do so forever. Soft, curvy hips rounding down to firm thighs, the small tattoo of a butterfly fluttering up her waist, the faint dusting of hair barely covering her sex. The images had been embossed into his memory and now it was all displayed before him, ready for his taking.

He doubted he'd last long enough for a simple touch.

Untwisting his tongue, he managed to utter, "You're so beautiful," in a way that made her smile. Maybe it was the tremor in his voice, or the heavy tent in his slacks. Whatever the case, the appreciative smile brought him joy, and propelled him into action.

While she sauntered to the bed and stretched herself over the duvet, he kicked off his shoes and got naked, remembering to pull the lone condom from his wallet before tossing his trousers on the chair. He wished he had more, quite assured by studying the sultry look in her eye that one time wouldn't be enough. But forcing himself to take first things first, he tossed it on the nightstand and stepped to the edge of the bed.

His cock stood hard and erect between them, removing any doubt she might have as to her effect on him. And when she eyed it unabashedly, her wicked smile nearly pushed him to the edge. She had the most enchanting bedroom eyes, bright and vivid blue, they somehow managed to look seductive yet vulnerable at the same time. They were inept at hiding her thoughts,

and what he saw in them ripped his mind of any trace
of reservation as he lowered to the bed and stretched
out next to her.

Her silky body caressed over him like satin sheets,
her legs snaking around his, her hands smoothing up
his back. If there was such a thing as pure perfection, he
now held it in his arms, and when he pressed his mouth
to those plump, rosy lips, their sweetness sent a bolt of
heat straight through him.

"Every inch of you is so tantalizing, I don't know
where to start," he admitted, taking a bare breast in his
palm to admire its virtues.

"That's a good place," she whispered, cupping her
hand over his.

He kissed his way toward the luscious mounds, savoring the smooth lines of her neck, the tender arc of her
shoulder, the flowery scent of her perfume. He didn't
let a spot go unexplored until his lips had reached her
nipple and he sucked it into his mouth.

She arched into him, those slim fingers digging into
his biceps and urging him to continue.

Her tender coos washed over him as he nibbled and
licked, the sexy moans inspiring him, her encouraging
hands slipping around his neck and holding him against
her.

"Suck harder," she begged, and he happily obliged,
circling one nipple with his thumb while he bit and
sucked the other.

She squirmed under him, her breath beginning to
labor until he abandoned her breasts to continue his
travels downward. He met the light and wispy butterfly
that hovered southeast of her navel, tracing it with his
tongue as he brushed his hands over her hips and down

her thighs, using all his senses to absorb and explore this beautiful woman.

His hand slipped around her knee and came back up her inner thigh, and when it neared the apex, she groaned and parted her legs in welcome.

The scent of sex wafted up and wrapped hold of him, surging more blood to his cock and trapping the air in his lungs. "You're going to undo me," he said as he dipped lower, his mind begging him to slow while his body begged him to hurry. He'd wanted to enjoy a tempered savor, to tease and torment until she sobbed for release, but when he touched a finger between her folds and was greeted with slick desire, he lost any chance at control.

She quaked and cried when he swiped his tongue between her flesh, the sweet taste starting a churning in his chest he'd never felt before. It was a guttural need to feel this woman unravel at his hand, to take possession of her body as a key to her soul. Like taming a wild horse and having it answer only to him, he wanted to learn how to lift her high and how to bring her down hard. But he doubted he could quell his own greed in order to do that thoroughly. She was too hot and he was too needy. So instead of mastering her in one session, he opted to take her in small courses, starting with how it felt to have her come against his lips.

He slid off the bed and knelt between her legs, spreading her wide and pulling her toward him until those glorious petals of flesh splayed open for him. And when she caught the intent in his eyes, a hazy smile curved her lips.

He smoothed a light finger over her hot wet clit, grinning when the strength left her body and she sank against the bed. He took alternate turns watching her then pressing light kisses to her thighs, circling his tongue around her flesh then watching her gasp and groan when he slipped a finger inside.

Her languid body surged when his thumb made contact with her sensitized nub, and when her gaze met his she mouthed the word, "Yes."

"You like that?" he teased. "How about this?"

He replaced his thumb with his tongue, swiping a long slow stroke across her clit as he lifted his finger and pressed it against her G-spot. Her body shook, the urgent groan from her chest sounding foreign and dire.

She slipped her fingers through his hair and arched toward him. "Please, don't stop now. It feels so good and I need it bad."

He wrapped his arm around her thigh and lifted it high, spreading her wider as he granted her request and took her into his mouth.

A hard shiver ran through her, spilling from her body into his as he sucked and licked, twirling his tongue in circles faster and harder until her fingers trembled and she broke in two. With a strangled moan the orgasm hit hard, gripping her tightly, her body pulsating against his lips until she let out a cry and began to buck and squirm. Her sharp release swelled his loin, sending such sharp sensation through him he feared he might come from the ecstasy of her release.

This was exactly how he knew it would be—hot and greedy, like no other sex he'd had before. And when her climax finally subsided and she lay sated on the bed, he decided it was time to move on to the next course.

Sheathing himself quickly, he lowered onto the bed, ready to spread her wide and take her. But before he could, she came to her knees and turned so her entrance faced him from behind.

"Take me this way," she urged, wiggling her ass.

Not one to argue, he leveled his thighs with hers, held her hips firm and slowly slid his throbbing cock into her hot, slick core. Smooth velvet coated him, draining any remnant tension from his neck, down his back and off his tired muscles. Her eager moan sang like music in his ears, and he pushed deeper, slow and steady until his waist hit the tender flesh of her ass and he couldn't go farther.

A curse slipped from his lips. This was too luxurious to bear, and knowing that the slightest stroke would throw him swiftly over the edge, he held steady for a while, bending over to toy with her breasts until the impending threat of climax calmed.

"I love the way you fill me," she said, pushing herself closer and sinking in just a little more. "I knew you'd fit just right."

He bent close to her ear and confessed, "If I dare move I'm going to come right now."

She giggled, and the vibration almost proved his words. "Then you'll just have to come again later."

"I've only got one condom."

"I've got more."

It was nice to know, but the embarrassment of quick release kept him in place, and instead, he dipped his fingers to her clit and began circling it slowly.

"Ohhhh," she moaned. "I like that."

And then as if to taunt him, she flexed her muscles and massaged his cock from inside.

"Oh, hell," he said, the feeling too glorious to try to discourage. And though he knew it would be the beginning of a quick end, he couldn't help but gently rock in rhythm with her moves.

"Yeah, keep stroking me," she urged, arching farther and spreading wider.

She reached a hand between them and grabbed his balls, sending a burst of sensation that gripped his jaw and tightened his spine. She stroked his sac over her heat while she rocked, pushing and squeezing those talented muscles to the point where all he had to do was hold on and enjoy the ride.

Though he wasn't foreign to women, he'd never experienced anything like this, and his fears of coming too soon took a backseat to the simple wonder of where all of this would end.

She nudged up, leaning into him until he was no longer kneeling but sitting on the bed, her body impaled on him from behind, her hands still gripping his balls and stroking them over her clit. She rocked and thrust, leaning her back against his chest while he brought his hands to her breasts and began toying with her taut nipples.

Wet sex encased him, steaming the blood in his veins as the slow burn began to take over. It started in his chest and twirled down his belly like a cyclone, building speed as it whipped toward the place where their bodies joined.

"Oh, babe, I'm going to come," he warned. But all she did was churn faster.

She pulled his hand from her breast to her sex. "Stroke me there, like you did before." And when he did, her labored breath told him she was just as near.

Once, twice, he twirled his fingers around her clit until her thighs flexed and her hands gripped tight for support. She ground against him, squeezing and rocking until the pressure reached the end and he couldn't hold on.

His shaky fingers barely registered her climax as he clamped his mouth to the nape of her neck and smothered a grunt of release. It took him over, thrusting his body up and over until she was no longer on his lap but bucking against him on all fours.

He gasped for air, the orgasm taking control of his body as he held on tight and drained into her.

In that instant, time stopped, awareness of anything but the rippling sensations lost in the ecstasy of the moment. He closed his eyes, urgent groans tangled in his throat, and only when the pulses began to subside did he discover he'd ended up nearly on top of her.

His hands were draped around her waist, holding her close while the heavy beat of his heart thumped against her back. They both wrangled for air, their lungs working hard to restore the oxygen in their blood. And then slowly and tenderly, he slid from her, turned her over and slipped by her side.

A trickling warmth slid through him when he felt her lips press gently against his chest. "I knew you'd be amazing," she said. And while he savored the compliment, he had trouble feeling as though he had anything to do with it. If that *Hush* magazine spread had etched her body onto his mind, this encounter in the flesh would seal her there for eternity. It was, without a doubt, the best sex he'd ever had. And they'd only gotten started.

He held her against him until the strength came back to his limbs and he was able to return her soft caresses and tender kisses. Their bodies meshed together like hand in glove, legs intertwined and hearts beating together while they rested and reflected on the encounter.

And when she finally spoke again, she looked

at him with that sexy worried brow. "No regrets, remember?"

He kissed her lips. "I confess, I have one." The worried brow darkened to anger, and before she could whop him, he tilted her chin and looked her in the eyes. "I regret that we didn't do this a week ago."

8
_____

"I'VE COME TO A CONCLUSION." Rachel set the garden salad she'd ordered from room service on the king-size bed then slid under the sheet next to Marc. "I've decided you're a way nicer guy without your clothes on."

Marc laughed heartily.

"See?" She pointed a finger as she fluffed a pillow and got comfortable. "That right there. It proves my point. I've been here over a week and this is the first time I've heard you laugh." Through a sultry smile, she added, "Do you know how sexy you are when you laugh?"

He scooted back and settled against the headboard, trying to decide whether he should be flattered, amused or insulted. He opted for turned on, not only from the bedroom look of her rosy cheeks and mussed-up hair, but by the unassuming way she had of speaking her mind. Marc had always appreciated that in a woman, though he had to admit he hadn't expected it from this one.

"No, I suppose I don't," he said, still chuckling.

She picked a slice of kiwi from the plate and slipped it between her lips, licking the juice from her finger in a casual move that shot straight to his cock. He wondered if she had any idea how much sex appeal she could pack in the simplest of gestures. Given the oblivious expression on her face, he gathered she didn't.

"You're a dreamboat when that dimple pops out and you flash those beautiful teeth," she said. "You should make it a permanent part of your uniform."

"I'll make a note of that."

He grabbed a carrot stick and took a bite while trying hard to get a fix on this curious woman. Her comments should have embarrassed him, but given the breezy way she'd made them, he couldn't find it in him. It was one in a long line of surprises she'd been tossing his way since she showed up at the resort.

From the beginning Rachel had been throwing him curves. When he'd concluded she was spoiled, she'd showed a tender caring side. When he'd labeled her pampered, she'd unveiled a strength that rivaled the toughest men. When he'd pegged her as a manipulative flirt, she'd leveled him with unabashed honesty.

Yet despite those sides of her, the spoiled, pampered flirt was still in there, adding enticing layers to a woman he was finding increasingly complicated.

"I mean, really," she said, rolling onto her side and propping her head in her hand. "You run a resort. That's got to be up there with personal shopper as one of the best jobs on the planet."

He nodded. "I suppose it is."

"Then why so glum all the time?"

The remark took him aback. "I'm not glum."

She snorted.

"I'm not," he defended. "The job keeps me busy, is all."

"Yes, Brett tells me you're all but married to the

place. And if it seemed you were having fun that would be one thing, but…" Instead of finishing the sentence she simply shrugged.

"I have lots of fun."

She scoffed. "*Brett* has lots of fun. And given his tennis career, I can see why he's here. *You,* I haven't been able to figure out."

Bugged by something he couldn't put his finger on, he finished his carrot and frowned. "What's there to figure out?"

"What you're doing here, for starters. How is it you ended up running a resort?"

He shrugged. "It's something I've always wanted. Ever since I was a kid on vacation, I wanted to find a place like this and stay forever."

"So you did a lot of vacationing when you were growing up."

He reached for a celery stick as he considered the question. "Two or three times a year, I suppose. My folks are both corporate executives. Our home life was always interrupted by last-minute business trips and conference calls. Between my mom and dad, one was always in the middle of some sort of big deal or corporate emergency. But a few times a year, the four of us got away, no faxes or telephones. All attention was on me and Brett. I think I grew up associating places like this with something special. As long as I can remember, I've always wanted to be a part of it on a permanent basis."

"And has it turned out to be everything you'd thought it would be?"

"Sure. Granted, it's a lot of work. Resorts don't run themselves. And with the partnership, investor reports need to be maintained, but still—" he waved a hand over the room "—look around. This place is beautiful. It's like working in paradise."

She made a face as if she didn't believe him.

"What?"

"You surprise me, that's all. I assumed you'd had your sights set on becoming the next big hotel magnate—nose to the grindstone, building your empire kind of guy. By seeing you on the job, I wouldn't have thought you were here because you wanted to spend your life basking in paradise."

"Well, no. There hasn't been much time for recreation. But I take the time to enjoy it all."

She made that disbelieving face again. "Right. When did you last have a day off?"

The gnawing annoyance came back. It seemed he'd unwittingly slipped into a petri dish and was about to be studied and analyzed. Or worse, end up on the receiving end of a ton of unsolicited advice.

He wasn't interested. He liked his life, loved what he did for a living and was proud of how far he'd come in his thirty-four years. What he didn't like was having to defend it or refute the idea that he might have missed something in his meticulously calculated plans.

"Christmas?" she asked when he didn't answer quickly enough.

Absently, he shook his head. "We're open on Christmas. People come here for the holidays. It's actually quite a big event—"

"You're kidding. You didn't even go home for Christmas?"

His aggravation welled. "My parents were just here in September—"

"You mean you skipped *Thanksgiving,* too?"

Pushing the platter to the side, she slid from the sheet

and straddled her naked body over his lap. "Mr. Strauss," she started, trailing a finger down his chest and flashing such a flirty, teasing smile that his annoyance quickly faded. "Or should I say, *Mista Scrooge,*" she added in a thick Cockney accent. "Hasn't anyone told you that all work and no play makes Jack a dull boy?"

"I, uh—ohh…" She lifted her hips and slid the sheet out from between them, leaving nothing between his cock and her hot silky bottom.

"Starting with this," she said, pointing to the celery stick he'd forgotten he'd been holding. "We've got this beautiful plate of lush fruit and vegetables and you reach for a celery stick?" She took the vegetable from his hand and held it in front of him. "Something tells me this is symbolic of the life you've been leading."

"What's wrong with celery?" he asked, his voice lurching when she wiggled her butt over his growing erection.

She tossed the green stick over her shoulder and picked a plump red strawberry from the plate. "*This* is life." Leaning close, she brought the berry to his mouth and fed him a bite. "This has flavor and color. It's sweet, a bit tangy." She bit her lip and gave him that languid *Hush* magazine smile that almost had him choking on the small bite.

He had to admit, the berry *was* much more delicious, though so would the celery have been if she'd fed it to him like this.

"You need to learn how to play, Jack," she whispered. Then she dragged the bitten end of the berry across his lips and moved in for a taste. "Mmm, see? You can't share sweetness like that with a dull stick of celery."

She closed her mouth over his, the essence of fruit mingling between them as they twirled tongues and savored kisses. Though they'd been in bed for hours, his body still responded as if they'd only gotten started. And while he didn't mind all the hours his job required, it did leave him suspecting he'd gone far too long without sex.

How else could he explain his insatiable appetite for this woman he shouldn't even be friends with, much less taking to bed?

The gentle shift of her body against his cock swept away his contemplation and pulled his thoughts back to what mattered right now—namely him inside her for however long it took to answer the lust in his system.

Breaking the kiss, she brought the half-eaten strawberry back to his mouth. "How about another taste?"

"I'd love one." But instead of taking a bite, he took the berry from her hand and smoothed the soft juicy end over her nipple.

RACHEL'S BREATH HITCHED when the cold berry made contact with her hot sensitive flesh. Hours ago, if someone had suggested Marc Strauss was this playful in bed, she would have laughed herself to tears. Sure, she'd had the hots for him from the start, had ached and fantasized about being exactly in this spot. But even in her fantasies, she'd accepted that he would probably be as business-driven between the sheets as he was in his office. This newfound revelation was a delight, and eagerly welcomed on a day when she'd so needed a lift to her spirits.

He slid his hand up her back and coaxed her breast to his mouth, circling his tongue around the spot he'd just sweetened with fruit.

"Mmm, you're right," he said. "Strawberries are delicious."

She chuckled, as well as she could through the sensation streaking through her, while he alternately traced the berry over her nipples with his tongue then licked the juice from her skin. It was euphoric, surges of pleasure, bliss and contentment twirling through her and leaving her with a feeling of well-being she hadn't experienced in a long time.

He rocked his hips and thrust his shaft against her waist, and she shifted so the hard flesh stroked against her sex. The man had a glorious body, firm runner's thighs and a toned chest and abs that were rigid. From the start, she'd marveled over how he looked in a suit, but today she got the extra bonus of enjoying the body underneath.

His gentle moans filled her ears like songs of praise while his tender touch worked her into another lusty storm. As she smoothed her clit along his shaft, her pulse skipped every time his hard cock twitched against her. She wanted it inside her again, wanted to look into those intense blue-gray eyes and make a connection that would last beyond this one night. She had three more weeks at this resort. How luxurious would it be to spend them all between the sheets like this?

He kissed the spot between her breasts then tossed the spent strawberry back on the platter. She assumed so they could move on to other things, but as he set the plate aside, he plucked a larger berry from the center of the plate.

He raised a brow and held it between them. "This one's been dipped in chocolate."

She liked the intrigue in those eyes. "It's for dessert."

"How convenient, since I'm ready to move on to the final course."

With the big plump strawberry pinched between his fingers, he nudged her off his lap and onto her back. Spreading her legs wide, he settled between her thighs. The fire in his eyes excited her, trickling more sensation to her throbbing sex, and when he touched the cold berry between her legs, a shiver ran from her fingers to her toes.

"Mmm." He smiled lazily and began circling the chocolate tip around her clit in a move that first aroused then tormented. And though she loved to watch as he stimulated her, the sumptuous feel of the cool pressure against wet heat had her sinking back against the mattress.

She sank against the fluffy down coverlet they'd kicked to the foot of the bed, surrounding herself in soft luxury while he stroked her into another frenzy. He dragged the berry around her clit, down lower then back again, whipping up sparks of electricity that arched her back and curled her toes. As much as she wanted him inside her, she couldn't deny the luscious feel his tantalizing moves produced. It filled the air with a fruity scent and teased her body into a cyclone of lust and desire.

"Hmm," he said. "The chocolate seems to be melting." He tossed the berry on the plate. "Don't want to make a mess." Kicking the platter to the side, he tucked his hands under her butt and dove in, moaning with delight as he touched his tongue to her sweet, sticky sex.

Air trapped in her lungs, the sharp pulses gripped her chest as that talented tongue went to work again, pushing her dangerously near another hard and satisfying release.

Bursts of heat overtook her as he licked and sucked,

his fingers caressing her flesh, his moans pushing her to the edge. And while the feeling was glorious, she was overcome with the need to share this release together, face-to-face, where she could study his eyes and make a connection that would take this intimate meeting beyond this one night.

Despite everything they'd shared this evening, she couldn't shake her fear over what she'd get tomorrow. Her spirit couldn't take any day-after regrets or Dear Jane speeches. She'd meant what she'd said earlier. She was finally beginning to like him. And now that she'd gotten a glimpse of the passionate side of this thorny man, she felt the need to make sure nothing sent them back to the stiff tension that had been hanging between them.

She tugged against his shoulders. "Please, come inside me."

He grunted and kept on going, but she squirmed and insisted, "No. I need you."

Obliging, he kissed a slow, torturous path across her thigh and down her leg as he reached for a condom from the side table. And before her body could calm from his succulent assault, he sheathed himself and settled over her.

She cupped his face and drew his gaze to hers, seeing nothing but raw passion and burning desire. It put a smile on her face as he lowered his mouth to hers and pressed a kiss to her lips. And when he filled her in one long steady stroke, an urgent need came over her, the sheer perfection snatching her breath and kindling that fear that wouldn't stop grating.

She wasn't sure where it came from. Maybe the joy of spending time with him coupled with her long history of disappointments. She'd grown accustomed to good things going bad, and though she hadn't intended to speak her mind, she heard herself say, "Tell me this won't be just tonight."

The instant she uttered the words she wished them back. Someday she'd learn to put a filter between her thoughts and her mouth. But this push and pull she felt around Marc had a habit of bringing out the best and worst in her. From the start, she'd adored yet hated him, ached for him then wanted him gone. And now that they'd found this peaceful union, she didn't want to lose it.

He smiled and kept stroking. "Can we talk about this later?"

She grabbed his hips and upped the speed, her body nearing climax despite the growing seed of anger that he hadn't given the answer she'd sought. "No. I need to know now."

He rose up on his palms and looked into her eyes. "What are you looking for, Rachel?"

She spread her hands over his chest and felt his heart. "Just friendship."

It seemed to ease the confusion in his eyes, and he slowly resumed his steady stroke. "Of course, you have my friendship." Bending down, he kissed her deeply. "What kind of man do you think I am?"

"Conflicted. That's what worries me."

He chuckled against her lips. "Maybe, but I'm not a jerk."

A smile broached her face. "I could argue that." Then she rocked in rhythm with him, slipping her hands back down to his hips and letting the sensation take over. "But I really like this. I don't want the old prickly Marc back again tomorrow."

Brushing his chin against her cheek, he kissed a

tender spot below her ear and whispered, "We need to keep this under wraps, you realize that."

"I can keep a secret."

He kissed her again then upped the pace. "Then we have an understanding."

He flung her leg over his shoulder and sank in deep, setting any further conversation aside in lieu of the heat building between them. She tried to hold on, wanted the two of them to seal their understanding with a climax that rocked them together, but her body had been too ready, the sensation too ripe.

With one last thrust, she broke apart, her fingers clinging to the bed like her heart clung to his promise that everything they had tonight wouldn't be gone tomorrow. It was silly, really. She didn't love the man, so she certainly shouldn't care. But history had shown her that all good things usually ended long before she wanted them to. In the week she'd been here she'd found tranquility and a sense of purpose she'd only begun to explore. This place and the people in it were becoming important to her, and the closer she got, the more frightened she became that it would all crash down around her.

But as her body succumbed to pleasure, those fears faded in the waves rippling through her, and when Marc's release followed hers, she slipped her leg from his shoulder and pulled him down against her chest. Together, they clutched and moved until the waves subsided and they were left spent and languid in a tangled mass.

She ended up spooned against him, the beat of his heart thumping a calming rhythm against her back. And as she relaxed in the warmth of his embrace, she reflected over this strange week that seemed to keep taking unexpected turns. After the encounter in Marc's office, she never would have believed they would end up here. And despite his assurance, she still wasn't convinced they would end up back here again.

Ever since she showed up at this resort nothing had gone as planned. Only a fool would believe that she could start controlling things now.

So as the shadows in the room began to darken and Marc's breathing slowed and quieted, she closed her eyes and decided to take this journey as it came, one day at a time.

If the previous week had taught her anything, it was that she really had no other choice.

9

"THIS IS OUR LAST ROOM." Anita rolled the housekeeping cart up to the door and glanced at her watch. "It looks like we'll be able to take off early. We could be out of here by two."

Rachel double-checked the room number on the list. "And it's not a checkout, so it should go pretty quick." That meant she might have time to squeeze in a full spa treatment before tonight when she hoped to catch up with Marc.

Excitement tingled in her belly. For over a week she'd been meeting him covertly after hours in either her suite or his on-site apartment overlooking the golf course. What had started as a night of uncontrollable passion had turned into a habit—one Rachel had no interest in kicking as long as she was stuck at the resort. The man was good for her body and her spirit. And much to her own amazement, even when they weren't burning up the sheets, she was finding that she actually liked him.

In the short time they'd spent together, she'd uncovered all kinds of surprising things about him, like the fact that he could cook, he loved classic movies, and had once won a talent contest by juggling bowling balls.

When she'd unpeeled the surface, Rachel had found a man very different from the one she'd expected. In fact, the more she got to know him, the harder it became to reconcile the man on the job with the one she met after hours.

And she couldn't wait for this evening to roll around so she could get to know him even better.

"You take the beds, I'll take the bathrooms," Anita said. She brusquely rapped on the door. "Housekeeping!"

After a brief pause, the women grabbed their supplies and entered the suite. This particular room was a two-bedroom suite with a king-size bed in one room and two doubles in the other. With twice the beds and bathrooms it would be more work than a standard single, but she and Anita had gotten good at whipping through double-speed.

Especially with a free afternoon on the horizon and all kinds of steamy ideas for her evening.

So without haste, she and Anita went their separate directions to get the job done. It was only after Rachel had finished the first bedroom and moved to the other that she realized they weren't alone. Sitting in a stuffy chair by the window was a young girl with headphones on her ears and her nose firmly planted in a book.

The sight took Rachel aback, not just from the shock of seeing someone she hadn't expected, but by the ghostly girl herself. She was classic Goth, with teased-up jet-black hair and dyed-red bangs, no older than fifteen or sixteen, Rachel guessed. Though her nails were painted black and her clothing was clearly punk, she had nothing visibly pierced, which either meant she was younger still or her parents weren't supportive of this chosen fashion style.

Rachel wondered why, with so much to do on such a beautiful day, the girl was sitting there alone in her suite, and as Rachel stepped into the room, she cleared her throat and got the girl's attention.

The girl casually glanced up, apparently not surprised by the intrusion, but her eyes slowly widened when she realized who was standing in her doorway.

"Hi," Rachel said. "I didn't know the suite was occupied. We can come back later if you prefer."

The girl pulled the headphones from her ears and stared, her eyes round as big blue gumballs. "No, um, that's okay."

Rachel began by emptying the wastebaskets then moved to one of the beds, all the while feeling the burn of the girl's gaze following her around the room.

"You're Rachel Winston," the girl finally said.

"That's me." Fluffing a pillow, she glanced over and smiled.

"I heard you were here, but no one I talked to had seen you."

"I've been trying to keep a low profile."

"This is too cool."

The girl reached into the pocket of her sweater and pulled out a cell phone, flipping it open in a gesture Rachel immediately recognized as a move to take a photo.

"Hey, don't do that," Rachel snapped. "Please."

The girl stopped and considered, neither clicking the photo nor putting the phone away. She seemed disappointed, though given her expression had barely changed since Rachel walked in, it was hard to tell for sure.

She sat contemplating for a moment but finally closed the phone without taking the picture. "It's just that the kids at school will never believe me." She tucked the phone back in her pocket.

Yes, that was definitely disappointment on her face, and as Rachel studied the girl, her heart tugged over an aura that felt rather sad.

"I'll tell you what," Rachel said. "Before I leave, I'll get my coworker, Anita, to take a picture of both of us together. How does that sound?"

A tiny smile curved her lips. "Cool."

Rachel went back to straightening the bed, working in silence until the girl uttered, "Didn't you, like, stab someone in a rage of fury?"

Rachel laughed and shook her head. "That one, I hadn't heard." Though she didn't make an attempt to explain what *had* happened. She wasn't about to take on the task of correcting every overblown story about her life. It would be a never-ending job. Instead, she diverted the subject by asking, "What's your name?"

"Rain."

Rachel smiled. "Nice to meet you, Rain."

She pulled the coverlet over the bed then stepped around to make sure it was even on all sides.

"It's really Renee, but I go by Rain. I'm going to have it legally changed when I turn eighteen."

"When will that be?"

"A couple years."

"Well, I like both names."

With the first bed done, Rachel moved to the second one closer to the window and the chair where Rain was sitting.

"What are you reading?" Rachel asked.

"A paranormal romance." Rain tossed the book on the table next to her. "It's kinda dumb. I like murder mysteries better." She began picking at her nails. "Do you read fiction?"

Rachel shook her head. "I'm dyslexic, so I never did much reading."

"No way!" Rain perked. "I am, too, but I read a lot. Didn't you have tutors? There's tricks you can learn that help, you know."

"I did, but not until I was nearly your age." And by then, she'd had no interest. School and grades had never been high priorities in the Winston household, but Rachel suspected that despite Rain's rebel appearance, they were probably priorities in hers.

"So, what are you doing here all alone? You must be here with family," Rachel asked.

Rain's bright almost-smile dimmed. "They're on some stupid Jeep tour."

"You didn't want to go?"

"It's all part of my brother's tennis tournament." She rolled her eyes. "Totally rank."

"Oh, your brother's in the tennis tournament going on here this week?" She'd remembered Marc telling her about it.

Picking the book back up, the girl opened it and went back to her reading. "Yeah."

Apparently, Rachel's interest in Rain's brother didn't go over well. "I take it you'd rather be doing something else."

Without looking up from the book, the girl shrugged.

Rachel went back to turning down the sheets on the second bed. "Is it just you and your brother?"

"We've got a little sister, Marcy. I'm in the middle."

Rachel nodded, not needing to hear much more in order to piece together the dynamics of the family. She could tell by the neatness of the rooms, the reading material dotted about and the few pieces of clothing that had been draped on the chairs. This was not a Goth family. On the contrary, Rain was most assuredly the self-proclaimed outcast in a preppie unit that probably idolized the tennis playing son.

Though just to be sure, she asked, "And I guess the family's making a big to-do about your brother's tennis career?"

"You'd think he was the next Andre Agassi."

"I'm sorry. That must be hard. I guess you two don't get along."

Rain blinked, taken aback by the question. "Gary? He's actually pretty okay." Then a fire hit her eyes. "And he's not the saint Mom and Dad think he is, though I'll never tell."

"You sound like a good sister."

She shrugged and went back to her book, prompting Rachel to continue working on the bed. She couldn't help feeling a connection to the girl. Maybe it was what they had in common, that feeling of being out of place in the world they were born into, of being on the sideline of their parents' lives when they really wanted to be in the center. Though Rachel had never competed against a sibling, she'd definitely competed against her parents' careers. And as was apparently the case with Rain, she'd ended up the loser.

"So you skipped the Jeep tour and decided to kick back here?"

"I'm skipping all of it, not that they care. They only dragged me here because they didn't want me home alone for the week. They figured I'd have a big kegger party. It just goes to show how much they know me—*not.*"

"You mean you wouldn't have had a wild party if you had the house to yourself all week?"

Rain looked up at Rachel with the same eye of frustration she probably gave her parents a hundred times. "No, I'm totally not into that. Not that you could tell *them* that."

At least it seemed that despite what they had it common, Rain was growing up with a better head on her shoulders.

"So while they're out celebrating their golden child," Rain grumbled, "I'm stuck here in this prison for the rest of the weekend."

"They'll be back soon, won't they? Those Jeep tours are only a couple hours."

"They've got all kinds of things going on. They won't be back until after the banquet dinner this evening."

"I'm sorry," Rachel said.

Rain shrugged. "No skin off my nose."

But Rachel could see that it was. She went back to finishing up the bed before moving to the main room, and while she worked, she thought about Rain and her family. She could almost picture the argument between her and her parents, the frustration from both sides where neither of them filled each other's ideals and expectations. At twenty-six, Rachel was old enough to understand the parents' concerns, yet still young enough to feel for Rain and her situation. Teenage years could be tough ones for a girl. It was the age where Rachel had started a long and painful downward spiral, of which she was still dealing with the obvious repercussions.

And as she considered what that had been like, she became bothered by the idea of simply saying her good-byes and walking out. Like so many experiences she'd had during her time at the resort, this was another that seemed to call to her. In another time and place, she wouldn't have given a girl like Rain a second thought. She would have been too wrapped up in her own issues to even notice.

But she wasn't in that place anymore. Here at this resort, she'd found the quiet to finally listen to the voice inside her, and this time the voice was telling her not to brush off the angry girl in the other room.

So when she and Anita finished up and got ready to leave, Rachel stepped back to the bedroom. "I was wondering," she said. "I'm off for the rest of the day. If it's okay with your parents, would you like to go check out the spa with me?" She held up her fingers. "I'm in need of a manicure. Maybe you could use one, too."

Rain's eyes brightened. "Really? You want me to hang with you?"

"You have to clear it with your folks."

Rain's excitement deflated. "They'll never believe me, and even if they did, they'll just say no."

"Give them a try. If they want, I'll talk to them myself."

Rain quickly dialed the number, and to her astonishment, her parents agreed to let her come with Rachel, as long as they didn't leave the grounds. As expected, Rachel had had to speak with them personally, and though Rain had been mortified, Rachel appreciated that they took such precautions with their daughter. They'd sounded like nice people who truly cared about her. Rachel suspected they simply weren't finding a space where they could connect with their rebellious child, and she hoped that someday they would.

In the meantime, she figured she could at least show the girl a good time this afternoon and give her something to go home and talk about. So with her new friend in tow, she took off to the spa.

They started off with manicures then made their way to the pedicure aisle where they slipped into adjacent massage chairs and soaked their feet in warm bubbling water. This was the first spa treatment Rachel had enjoyed since leaving Los Angeles, and after all the work she'd endured, the task she once took for granted now felt exceptionally luxurious.

Several people looked at the two of them curiously, one or two actually spoke up and said hello, but spending time in the public areas of the resort wasn't turning out to be the disaster Rachel had feared. It occurred to her that without the protection of Stefan, she'd virtually turned herself into a hermit. And while she did need to take caution with her public appearance while she was here, she hadn't needed to hole herself up in confinement for a month.

"This is so cool," Rain said, studying the silver-tipped French manicure she'd chosen. "I'm so glad I didn't go on that stupid outing with my folks."

The comment needled at Rachel, particularly in light of all the things she'd learned from Rain while having their nails done. It sounded like Rain idolized her older brother and that the two of them were close, but as Rachel had suspected, Rain's parents conflicted her by placing the boy on a pedestal. Rain had never been as smart or athletic as the older boy, which seemed to be okay until her younger sister was born, stripping her niche as the only girl in the family.

Rachel felt for her, but also knew from experience that there were always two sides to the coin.

"Now, come on," Rachel said. "If I hadn't come along, would it have really been better spending the day cooped up in that room? I've been on those Jeep tours, and they're pretty fun."

Rain frowned as though she were being lectured, leaving Rachel suddenly feeling very old. But maybe it *was* time to grow up a little. "Have you ever told your parents what bothers you about them?" she asked.

Rain huffed. "Constantly. Like it does any good."

"I think it's important you keep trying. Maybe if saying it one way isn't working, try a different approach."

"It doesn't matter. Gary and Marcy will always be the kids they salivate over, and I'll always be…not."

"It's possible that they simply have an easier time understanding Gary and Marcy. That doesn't mean they care any less about you. It only means you have to try harder to connect than the others."

Rain rolled her eyes. "Why bother?"

"Because they're all you've got. And like it or not, they'll always be important to you, even if you don't want them to be." She lowered her voice when the pedicurist sat down in front of her and began removing the polish from her toenails. "You know what I learned only recently? Parents are just people. They don't have all the answers, and some of them can be as messed up as the rest of us."

The comment brought out a faint smile.

"For me," she went on, "it was upsetting to discover they weren't the heroes I grew up thinking they were. But at the same time, once I figured that out, I stopped being so frustrated. Once I realized they were just as flawed and confused as I was, I started understanding them a little better, and stopped blaming them for everything."

Rain didn't answer, but Rachel could tell that her words might be resonating just a tiny bit. And given their short-term friendship, she figured that was enough. This was about showing a young girl a good time, not sending her through psychotherapy, so from that point on, she steered their conversation back to television and music and the kids at Rain's school.

After pedicures, they went for facials which did wonders for Rain's complexion by simply washing off all the harsh makeup and restoring the pretty girl underneath, if only for a while. Then the two decided to check out the shopping plaza that stretched between the main hotel and the banquet area of the resort where most of the weddings and conventions took place. They explored all the shops, talked about fashion, and sampled the delicious chocolates at Desert Desserts. It was well into the dinner hour when they finally collapsed into chairs at the terrace café and ordered two iced coffees.

Though it had only been a few weeks since Rachel had been out and about, it felt refreshing to go on a shopping spree and treat herself to a few luxuries that she used to take for granted. Especially in the company of someone like Rain, who seemed to be experiencing the fun of a girls' day out for the first time.

Sipping her coffee, Rain pulled a bright red tote from the bag next to her chair and admired it. Rachel had seen her ogling it in one of the stores and had treated her with the gift, buying a teal green one for herself in the process.

"My friend Audrey is going to be so jealous," Rain gushed. "This is the coolest bag ever."

"It is cool. I've got a tan pantsuit at home that needed this," Rachel said, admiring her new bag.

"So what next?" Rain asked. Her blue eyes were so bright and filled with cheer, Rachel wished it was Rain's mother sitting here enjoying the time with her daughter.

The girl Rachel was looking at now barely resembled the one she'd walked in on hours ago, and it left her sad to know that tomorrow this would all most likely revert back to the way it was.

Families had a way of doing that to people.

"Have you gone to Sammy 8's?" Rain asked.

"What's that?"

"It's the restaurant down by the tennis courts. They make all these wild things like dessert that looks like sushi and these exotic salmon tacos. You can see the chef cooking from your table, and every time a plate is ready, he flashes this neon sign and yells, 'Diiiiishhh!' We haven't gone, but I heard some people talking about it."

Just then, Rachel's cell phone rang. She pulled it from her purse and a tingle of excitement came over her when she saw that it was Marc. Ever since she'd snuck out of his apartment in the wee hours this morning, she'd been aching to get back. She hoped he was as interested in seeing her again, too.

"Excuse me for a second," she said, then quickly flipped the phone open. "Hello?"

"I've missed you," said the sexy voice on the other end of the line.

It spread a smile across her lips and warmed several parts of her body. Amazing, how all the man had to do was speak to turn her on.

"Me, too," she said.

"I need to make some last-minute checks on tomorrow's tournament, but after that, my evening is free." His voice lowered to something sultry. "Any ideas on how I might spend my time?"

She giggled like a schoolgirl. "About a hundred."

"How about you drop by my place in about a half

hour? We can order in. A couple John Wayne classics came in the mail the other day. I haven't checked them out yet. That is, if we get that far." He chuckled.

Nothing sounded better than another sumptuous evening with Marc, and she opened her mouth to accept when she caught sight of Rain's face and the eager look of anticipation in her eyes. Clearly, Rain wasn't ready to let their adventure end just yet, and as Rachel sat there with her mouth open, ready to give an answer, she imagined having to tell the girl that their fun afternoon had just come to an end.

"Rachel, you there?" Marc asked when she didn't answer.

"Uh, yeah."

Quickly, her mind recited the goodbye speech she'd give the girl then imagined sending her back to her room to have dinner alone while she waited for her family to return. All it did was remind Rachel of all the times she'd spent with her mother, only to be brushed off long before she'd wanted their day to end.

That kind of disappointment was all too familiar. While she'd ultimately learned to accept her mother for who she was, it was often when growing up that Abigail would whisk into town, pull Rachel out of school to spend a day of shopping and fun, only to dump her back at home hours later because something better had come along.

And as Rachel sat there staring at the unwitting smile on Rain's face, she didn't have the heart to do the same, even though she knew she hadn't made the girl any promises.

"Rachel? You okay?" Marc said.

The lusty thrill in Rachel's gut sank. "Hold on a second."

Holding the phone away, she turned to Rain. "Do you want to check out the restaurant tonight?"

The girl beamed. "Could we?"

"Under one condition."

"Anything!"

"Make me a promise that you'll go to your brother's tournament tomorrow and cheer him on."

The happy look in Rain's eyes dimmed.

Rachel sighed. "Rain, you love your brother. I know you do."

"Sure, but…"

"So even though your parents are totally annoying, don't you think your brother would appreciate it if you went to his tournament? I thought he meant a lot to you."

"I suppose."

"If you promise me you'll go cheer him on tomorrow I'll treat you to Sammy 8's tonight."

It took Rain about a half a second to agree. So with her spirit both pleased and disappointed, Rachel brought the phone to her ear and uttered to Marc, "Sorry. I'm going to have to pass."

10

"IN THE EYES OF THE LAW, this would be considered cruel and unusual punishment." Marc took a seat next to Rachel on the café terrace and lowered his voice to just above a whisper. "First, you ditch me for the night, and now that I finally get to see you again, it's in a place where I can't put my hands on you."

Rachel giggled and sipped her drink as if she hadn't a care in the world, which grated on him. He'd spent too much of last night feeling the weight of an empty bed, wishing she was with him like some pathetic lovesick teen. He'd missed her, both her body and her company, and had wanted to get back to their cozy den as quickly as possible. Yet when the day was through and she'd said she wanted dinner on the plaza instead of their private retreat, he'd stuttered, paused, then lapped it up accepting anything he could get.

How ironic that he'd spent so much time worrying that Rachel would wrap the staff around her finger, when in the end he was the first man to succumb to her.

"We've got all night," she said jovially.

"And I'd planned on making use of it."

Their server approached the table with a menu for

Marc, and after taking Marc's order for iced tea, went off to fetch the drink.

Over the rim of her glass of white wine, Rachel eyed him seductively. "I can't wait to see what you have in mind."

"My feelings exactly. So why don't we ditch this place and dine in?"

"Because it's time you got out and enjoyed your own resort for a change."

He opened his mouth to tell her he was enjoying it just fine behind closed doors when the server returned with his tea and asked if they'd like to order. Intent on getting this over as quickly as possible, he picked up his menu to toss out whatever he saw first, but Rachel took it from his grasp and set it on the table.

"We'd like a little time, please," she said, blinking those big blue eyes so sweetly that the man nearly tripped over his feet as he stumbled away.

Marc understood the sentiment. He'd spent a week sharing his bed with Rachel in the hope that somewhere during that time, the newness would wear off, his infatuation with her would temper and he might be able to go an hour in his day without thinking about her. They'd had more sex in seven days than he'd had in his life, but instead of getting old and familiar, it only seemed to get more exciting.

He'd hoped to sex her out of his system and get his focus back on the job and his resort, but the plan had blown up in his face. And now he'd surrendered to simply take what he could get before she packed up and went home to L.A.

"When was the last time you relaxed and enjoyed this beautiful resort?" she asked.

"I was enjoying myself very much night before last. And the night before that."

He could tell by the look on her face she was intent to spend some time here, so in a gesture of defeat, he slipped off his suit jacket, draped it over the chair and made himself comfortable, earning a satisfied smile from his temporary lover.

"Before yesterday, I'd spent over two weeks hiding out in my room," she said. "That is, when I'm not being guarded by the housekeeping staff. And while some of that time has been quite enjoyable—" she flicked a brow "—it occurred there was a beautiful resort here that I hadn't explored."

"From what you said earlier, it sounded like you had a good time yesterday."

"Well, I definitely missed spending time with a special someone, but it got me thinking. I've only been hiding out here for two weeks. *You've* been hiding for three years."

This was all coming clear to him. A continuation of the you-work-too-hard conversation she'd started a week ago. He'd thought he'd taken her mind off that track. Apparently, he'd only been able to sideline it. "All work and no play makes Jack a dull boy," he droned.

"If you were going to bury yourself in your work, you might as well have been a lawyer or an accountant." She waved a hand across the terrace, gesturing across the large courtyard of shops and cafés. The plaza truly was a beautiful place, shaded by palm trees and brought to life with large stone beds of flowers, greens and sturdy sculpted fountains.

When Marc and the partnership had bought the aging resort, they'd dumped hundreds of thousands into restoring the plaza to the beauty of its original heyday back in the fifties. And as he followed Rachel's gaze, he was reminded of just how spectacular it had all turned out.

"When was the last time you sat in one of these chairs, mingled with the guests, and enjoyed the paradise you've got here?"

"I have business meetings here all the time," he said absently as he looked upon a man and woman hand in hand with a young child. The girl ran to one of the fountains and stuck her chubby little hand in the water like the children always did, and her father knelt down and handed her a coin to toss in for a wish.

It was a sweet scene. The kind that reminded him of the life he hoped to have someday once he secured his future and was ready to settle down.

When Rachel didn't respond, he looked back and caught her skeptical expression.

"I wasn't referring to business meetings," she said. "I was referring to really sitting here and enjoying the food and the scenery around here. You know, that working-in-paradise thing you were talking about?"

He studied her. Gave it a long note of consideration. Came up with nothing. "Okay, so maybe you've got a point."

She laughed, a light whimsical sound that he'd heard a number of times in the darkness of their bed. He liked the way it sounded, especially when it came from her naked body pressed against his. And it reminded him that while he appreciated her sentiment, he would much rather be having it in a place where they didn't have to pretend to be mere acquaintances.

Sitting next to her like this, her silky thigh within reach, her familiar scent of lavender perfume drugging his senses, he might as well be in a torture chamber for lack of being able to touch her. His hand begged to reach out and stroke that soft skin, his lips tingled for the taste of her, not to mention all the other body parts aching to mingle with hers.

Unfortunately, he knew what he was up against, had seen that unbending stubborn side of her and knew, whether he liked it or not, Rachel was having her way tonight.

Reaching casually for the menu, he picked it up and agreed, "Okay. Beer and dinner on the terrace, and I promise to enjoy every minute of it."

She smiled with satisfaction and picked up her own menu just as Brett's voice sounded behind them.

"If I didn't see it with my own eyes I wouldn't have believed it."

Marc turned to find his brother approaching their table arm in arm with the woman he'd been dating the past couple weeks.

"My brother having dinner with a beautiful woman," Brett went on. He glanced at Rachel with the smirk he'd been perfecting since the third grade. "What is it, charity night?"

He clapped Marc on the back as Margaret held a quick hand out to Rachel. "Hi, I'm Margaret O'Dell. It's such an honor to meet you," she gushed. "I've been a fan of you and your mother for years."

Rachel eyed Marc then accepted the handshake.

"Are you two about to have dinner?" Margaret asked. "We were just looking for a bite to eat ourselves, weren't we, Brett?" Without waiting for him to respond, she added, "Maybe we could join you!"

Marc would sooner have a root canal than extend this dinner into a long drawn-out foursome, but with Brett already pulling out a chair and Rachel moving her purse from the vacant seat it didn't look as if he had an option.

He only hoped that when this was over and he got Rachel back to his room she was prepared for the long night of lovemaking he had in store for her.

JUST WHEN SHE'D FEARED her expensive dirt-searching venture would end up a bust, Margaret took a seat at the table, barely containing her excitement at running into Rachel in a rare public appearance—with Marc Strauss, no less.

This assignment had started out so promising, with rumors of tension between the convict celebrity and sexy hotel owner, followed by that sensational photo shoot in the hotel room she'd managed to orchestrate. Who'd known that stealing a few cleaning products off Rachel's housekeeping cart would result in a chain reaction of such brilliant calamity? She'd had to pay her poor photographer for the repair of the camera, in addition to a pricy bottle of Scotch for his trouble, but the end result had been worth it. Her editor was thrilled, and more important, eager to keep her credit line open to cover the rest of her stay here.

Unfortunately, from that moment on, all activity had come to a screeching halt. The housekeeping staff had put the clamps on Rachel, not only keeping her locked behind closed doors, but cynically questioning every guest who came down the aisles of the rooms she was cleaning. They'd flocked around her on breaks and sounded the alarm on any reporter caught snooping around.

It was as if the woman had created an entourage of secret service out of the hotel staff, all of them staunchly loyal to her—for what? The few pounds of imported chocolate she'd brought into the break room last week? Or was it the literary agent she'd put in touch with Anita Cooper, Rachel's partner in housekeeping who was apparently trying to get a book published?

According to Brett, the entire staff was ready to appoint Rachel to sainthood, which Margaret knew had foul written all over it. No way were so many people that tight-lipped, which meant Rachel was either being kept in near-total isolation, or she genuinely hadn't done anything scandalous since she'd shown up here.

And if Margaret knew anything about Rachel Winston, she'd bet her money on the former every day of the week.

There was no way Rachel could go into seclusion like this without doing *something* newsworthy. Margaret simply had to get close enough to find out what it was. She'd heard from several sources that Rachel had come out of hiding yesterday, which gave Margaret just enough of a carrot to keep her editor from pulling the plug on this assignment. Now, thanks to the lover she'd taken on for the sake of her story, those nights with Brett might be finally paying off.

"So, what has you two sharing dinner on the terrace tonight?" she asked.

Marc and Rachel shared a glance.

"I, uh…" Marc fumbled.

"Mr. Strauss was gracious enough to escort me out tonight," Rachel quickly kicked in. "I've spent so much time cooped up in my room, I was going stir crazy."

"Really," Margaret said, darting her eyes between the two. "I would have thought plenty of your friends would be visiting during your stay. After all, it's a public resort—a lovely one at that—and it's not like you're under house arrest. I've been hoping to do a little star gazing but I haven't seen a soul."

Rachel studied her with slightly more intrigue in her eyes than Margaret would have given her credit for. Maybe Rachel wasn't as dim-witted as she'd suspected—an early warning that Margaret would have to play her hand more carefully.

"We'd asked the Winstons that they keep Rachel's stay under the radar," Marc said. "Given the trouble we've had with the press, the addition of more celebrity guests would have made it difficult for us to protect Miss Winston's privacy."

"Of course," Margaret said.

"Which means poor Marc is having to babysit me," Rachel added, taking a sip of her wine. "He's being such a good sport."

The look she shot Marc carried a punch Margaret didn't miss, but instead of following it, Margaret rolled the conversation back to Brett and his tournament, careful not to come on too strong too fast. This was the golden opportunity she'd been working toward, and she wasn't about to blow it by letting her excitement get the best of her.

"How is the tournament going, by the way?" Marc asked. "All's been pretty quiet on my front. I haven't been fielding any major emergencies."

"It's been great," Brett said. "We had a couple players drop out at the last minute, but we were able to shuffle the brackets pretty easily and stay organized."

"Oh!" Rachel said. "How did Gary do today?" She tapped her finger on her glass. "Darn, what's his last name? Lesnansky! Gary Lesnansky." Turning to Marc, she said, "He's the brother of Rain, the girl I spent the afternoon with yesterday."

"Gary Lesnansky," Brett repeated. "He got knocked out of the semifinals this afternoon, but he did better than they'd expected considering his experience."

"That's good," Rachel said. "I sure hope Rain went to his tournament like I asked."

"Knowing teenagers?" Marc said. "I'd give it a fifty-fifty chance."

She frowned and shoved him playfully. "Stop being such a cynical snot."

He held up his hands. "You're the one questioning it."

"Children, children," Brett said, "Try to get along."

"Yes, Marc," Rachel teased. "Be nice to me."

There went another look, and this time Margaret knew for a fact there was something going on between these two. The air around the table practically reeked with innuendo, and though Marc tried hard to hide it, he couldn't keep his eyes off Rachel. If he wasn't already sleeping with the woman, he certainly wanted to.

Margaret spent the next hour studying them, watching every move while they enjoyed the French-California cuisine and chatted about everything from the tournament to the rich history of the Clearwater Springs Resort. As much as Margaret could get away with, she steered the conversation to how Rachel was spending her time here, but Rachel was far more poised at dodging any pointed questions than Margaret had expected.

It was unnerving, really. She'd never met Rachel personally. Had only made assumptions based on her shallow-minded blogs and that preposterous reality show she'd starred in briefly. What she hadn't expected was someone a lot sharper in the flesh than she appeared on screen, and it left Margaret with the grim reality that her fight to get a story might be harder than she previously thought.

"What's your mother been doing these days?" Margaret asked when the conversation hit a lull. "I was such a huge fan of Abigail, but I haven't heard anything about her in months."

"She's been abroad for a while now," Rachel said. "She was doing advertising for Paola, a line of clothing for older women, and has decided to stay on longer. Apparently, she's fallen in love with Italy and wants to buy a house there. I'm thinking about flying out and staying with her for a break when I'm done here."

Marc shot a quick glance at Rachel. "I didn't know that."

Rachel shrugged. "I haven't decided for sure."

Margaret watched as Marc set his fork on his plate and took a swig of his beer.

Everything in her said there was something going on between Marc and Rachel, but did she have enough to phone her editor and start a rumor? Photos. She needed photos.

Or even better, she needed this lover of hers to start helping out by digging into his brother's business. When she'd first approached Brett, she'd been under the impression the two men were close. And why wouldn't she? They'd gone into business together. They spent all day every day running this resort and all the activities the resort sponsored. She'd expected them to spend more time together, but in two weeks, all she'd managed to get out of Brett was that the two had been busy lately.

She needed him to start asking questions.

So when their dinner was finally over and she and Brett went their own way, she didn't waste any time.

"Those two are sleeping together."

Brett shot out a laugh. "What?"

"Marc and Rachel. I'd stake my career on the fact that those two are doing the bedroom tango after hours."

Brett gazed at her as if she had geraniums growing out of her ears. "That's ridiculous."

"I have eyes, and so do they. Those two couldn't keep them off each other all night."

He shook his head. "You don't know my brother. He'd never do something as stupid as sleeping with Rachel. In fact, he'd given me the long lecture of not sleeping with her myself last month."

Thinking he'd offended her, he quickly wrapped his arm around her shoulders and pecked her on the cheek. "Not that I'd even been thinking about it. I'm one gentleman who prefers blondes."

"Well, I think you're wrong. I'm a woman. We have intuition about these things and my intuition was screaming pretty loud and clear." When he tried to scoff it away, she pressed. "You should at least ask him about it, and if it's true, tell him to be more careful out in public. I mean, if I picked up on it, think about how horrible it would be if a reporter did, too. You wouldn't want that, would you?"

"No, but…" He looked down and saw the seriousness in her eyes. "All right. I'll ask him. But I'll bet you sexual favors that you've got this one all wrong."

She smiled. "Okay, sailor. You're on."

11

"I THOUGHT I'D NEVER get you here," Marc said, pulling the zipper on Rachel's pale pink dress as he nipped and kissed a path down the nape of her neck. "That was the longest, most torturous dinner I've ever had to sit through."

She chuckled and wiggled out of her clothing, the gentle brush of her ass against his waist stroking places that didn't need any more encouragement. He was already rock-hard, had been through most of dinner, and now that he'd finally gotten her back to her suite he didn't need much in the way of foreplay.

He wrestled off his shirt and tie as Rachel worked on his pants, his cock springing up when she yanked down his briefs and sent them sliding to the floor.

"Poor baby," she teased, tracing a finger along his shaft and giving him that *Hush* magazine pout that nearly brought him to his knees.

He'd never met a sexier woman in his life, definitely not one who held such carnal control over his body. She was like a narcotic, every taste of her only leaving him needing more, and after going a whole day without, his body felt as though it were in the throes of withdrawal.

This wasn't good. From the start, he was supposed to be getting the woman out of his system, not letting her sink in. But from the moment she'd set foot on his resort, nothing had been going the way he'd planned.

"What can I do to make it up to you?" she asked, but before he could answer, she clasped her fingers around his erection, whisking the words from his throat.

She pressed her mouth to his chest, kissing hot rings of fire everywhere her lips made contact with his skin. She licked his nipple, toyed with it then bit at his flesh while she used her fingers to gently stroke his eager cock. It was ecstasy and agony rolled into one, and while he wanted to move her to the bed and take control, his feet froze in place, not a cell in his body willing to move away from her luscious feast.

"You're already forgiven," he said, his limbs weakening as she trailed her talented mouth farther down his chest.

"You can't be that easy," she teased. "I've been such a bad girl. Surely, there's something I can do."

She dropped to her knees, sending a bolt of anticipation through him without so much as a touch. And when she pressed her lips to the head of his penis and gave it a tender kiss, he had to snake his fingers through her hair to stay afoot.

"That works," he said, the words lurching from his chest when she opened wide and sucked him like a lollipop. Sensation sped through him, the slippery velvet of those lips ripping away his thoughts and draining a day's worth of problems off his shoulders.

Oh, what a way to round out an evening, to take all the stress and worry and shove it out the door, leaving him calmed and thoroughly relaxed. It was an experience he was getting used to. And as she licked and stroked the tension from his limbs he became aware of his growing aversion toward letting it go.

Rachel was getting to him. Not just with a beautiful body and mind-blowing sex, but in the spirit of who she was and the things she'd brought to his life. She wasn't what he'd expected, and the more he got to know her, the more this affair between them became something more than simple lust.

Suddenly, his thoughts disappeared when she clasped his balls and licked him from tip to base. This wasn't going to last. He'd spent two hours watching her at the dinner table and fantasizing about getting inside her body. If she wanted more than short and sweet, they'd need to take a less direct route. So he attempted to pull away, but when he did she wrapped her hands around his thighs and yanked him back.

"No," she said. "This is good." Smiling, she looked up at him, those big blue eyes filled with purpose and sin. "I want it all the way." Then she opened wide and sucked him into her mouth.

He wanted to argue, would have if he hadn't spent two hours watching her eat her meal and wishing every morsel had been a part of his body. But when she moaned and took him in, all his restraint collapsed under the weight of that glorious mouth wrapped around him.

She licked him hard, stroking faster and gripping him firmer until his legs shook and his body exploded. And when he came, she palmed him, holding his cock against her chest where he spilled himself over her breasts.

She lolled her head back and groaned. "This is so hot." She used one hand to smooth the cum over her nipples while the other pumped out every ounce she could get from him. He grabbed her breasts and stroked his shaft between them, letting the smooth slippery mounds pull out the last of the climax while the heady scent of sex grew heavy in the air.

It was erotic and sexy, the waves continuing to ripple through him as he watched her stroking her own breasts. So much so that by the time the climax eased and his strength returned, he was already aroused and gearing up for another round.

He guided her to her feet and held her tightly, closing his mouth over hers and sinking into a long and greedy kiss. "You're amazing," he whispered before twirling his tongue around hers then taking her to bed. It was an understatement, and he knew it. A feeble attempt at avoiding trying to label what was really growing in his heart. But it was all he could give.

Because when he really looked close at what this woman was doing to him, he saw something he wasn't anywhere near ready to face.

"MY FEET ARE KILLING ME." Rachel slipped off her smock and tossed it in the laundry.

"It's always like this when the big tournaments clear out," Anita replied. She pulled her purse from her locker and dug for her car keys. "And with Jolie assigning us twice the rooms, I guess our easy ride was officially over."

No kidding. With the tennis tournament ending, half the resort checked out at once, leaving their day full of rooms needing top-to-bottom cleaning. It was safe to say that after three weeks, Rachel had finally gotten a real feel for the job. It was dirty and hard, and though she still enjoyed the camaraderie she'd developed with the people she'd met here, cleaning rooms was one thing she wouldn't miss when her service was over.

Of course, it hadn't helped that she'd gotten a thorough workout from Marc last night. When he'd gotten her back to her suite, he'd been nearly insatiable, ravaging her body like a sailor returning from six months at sea. Not that she was complaining. If there was a reason to wake up tired and drained, an endless night of sex with a hot and horny hunk was a pretty good one.

"At least we've got a weekend before we're back," she said. "See you Monday?"

Anita gave her a friendly hug. "Go soak those feet."

Rachel chuckled. "I'm going to soak everything."

Her smile lingered as she made her way out of the employee lounge, reflecting on the night she and Marc had shared and hoping tonight might bring more of the same. Though Rachel hadn't been short on lovers, she'd never had anyone like him. He knew all the right buttons to push, working her body as though he'd been studying her for years. But it wasn't only his talent in bed that set him apart. He was the first man who'd ever really made her feel as if he was there just for her.

Back in L.A., everyone had an agenda, be it a lead to her parents, the wealthy lifestyle she offered, quick fame or a photo in the celebrity magazines. But with Marc it was only her, and it was a reality that made her giddy, but sad.

Every day she spent with him was one day closer to the end of her stay, and as that day approached, she wished more and more that it would never come. She could easily admit to falling for him if she allowed herself to be real with her heart. She wouldn't, of course, knowing that accepting her feelings would only make it harder to walk away when it was time to go. And if she'd learned only one skill during her adult life, it was how to guard against the disappointment that the men in her life brought with them.

Over the years, she'd gotten good at keeping things casual, accepting that caution went a long way in protecting her heart. But the more time she spent here, the harder it became to hold her emotional distance. Everything about this place felt right, including her secret lover. And when she let her hopes wander, she could swear he'd felt it, too. She'd seen it in his eyes, the way he looked at her when they made love, and the way those early hungry kisses had turned tender over the past few days.

And when the night was quiet and her thoughts were loud, foolish voices had begun to ask if there was a way this all could last.

Pushing through the heavy wood door that led to the back gardens, she brushed off the thought and stepped into the sunlight, taking a long breath of sweet evening air to get rid of the silly ideas in her head. These were dangerous thoughts and she knew it. It was a fantasy, thinking she had a permanent place here. Keeping the press and the gawkers off the property was a strain that took resources, and she knew she was more a burden than a help. But this was the first time she'd really felt as if she belonged to something, and despite trying to keep her head about her, it was hard to keep the fantasies at bay.

"Hey, wait up."

The sound of Brett's voice jerked her from her thoughts and she turned, welcoming the distraction.

"Hey yourself."

"Done working for the day?" he asked, striding up

to her side. With the tournament wrapping up today, he wore a Clearwater Springs polo shirt and pressed slacks. It was very preppy and corporate, a look Rachel knew he only brought out of the closet when he had to.

"I'm done working for the rest of my life," she joked. "You really need to double the salaries of everyone on the housekeeping staff. They work harder than you can imagine."

He flashed his signature grin. "When Marc and I make our first million, we'll do that."

"I spent my day cleaning up after all those people you and your tournament brought in. Some of them were pigs, you know."

"Oh, I've heard stories, trust me. Speaking of the tournament, I was cornered by Mrs. Lesnansky today."

"Rain's mom?"

He nodded. "They were on their way out, but before they left, she wanted me to make sure I passed along her sincere thanks for what you did for Rain."

"I only took the girl shopping."

"I guess you did more than that. Her mom said after spending the day with you, she'd stopped sulking in the room, cheered her brother on at the tournament and even took her younger sister swimming. Mrs. Lesnansky seemed to think it was thanks to you."

"Really?" A smile crossed her face at the thought of Rain maybe taking some of her words to heart.

"Yeah. So, what exactly *did* you tell the girl?"

"That good or bad she was stuck with her family and might as well get along."

Brett laughed. "That simple, huh?"

"In a nutshell. Though I bought her an expensive purse to go along with the advice. Maybe she figured she owed me."

"Well, they were smitten with you and wanted to make sure I let you know how much they appreciated it. Cornered me and Marc this morning before they left."

"Thanks for telling me. That made my afternoon."

"No problem." He folded his arms over his chest and chomped away at his gum, eyeing her up and down as though there was more to say.

"Was there something else?" she asked, not sure what to make of the assessing look.

"It seems a lot of people around here are smitten with you," he finally said. "Even my own big brother."

She blinked, not sure where that came from or where it was going. "That's nice to hear."

"You two have gotten pretty cozy lately, huh?"

Okay, so it was going right where it shouldn't. She decided it was time to start walking. "I don't know what you're talking about."

He moved to keep in step with her. "Aw, c'mon, Rach. You can be real with me. What's going on between you and Marc?"

She tossed him a casual frown as they made their way down the main garden path. That wasn't a question she cared to grace with an answer, but she knew ignoring him was about as futile as herding cats. So she mentally worked up her most convincing denial when she rounded the corner and saw the preparations for a wedding ahead.

"Ooh, is someone getting married?"

Over a hundred bright white chairs were lined up on the grass facing a luxurious fountain surrounded by orange and lemon trees and rows of colorful roses. Though she'd been past this spot a dozen times, she hadn't seen it set up like this, and always a sucker for weddings, she couldn't help but stop and ogle.

Caterers dressed sharply in black and white were setting up what looked like a giant champagne fountain. A maintenance crew was fiddling with lights and a half dozen people scampered about, shuffling between the area outdoors and a large buffet room inside. Three sets of French doors joined the two spaces, and as eager to check it out as she was to dodge Brett's questions, she stepped inside to see what else was going on.

What looked like an acre of tables made a U-shape around a large maple dance floor. At the head of the room, maintenance workers and waitstaff were setting up what would no doubt be the long bridal table. Behind it, technicians were readying the stage for a band that hadn't yet arrived, and off to the side a mile-long buffet table was being formed.

"Come on, Rachel," Brett said. "Don't dodge the question."

"I love weddings," she said, ignoring Brett intentionally, though it wasn't a lie. She really did love them, especially this part where all the details were being pulled together and the room was abuzz with anticipation. She'd helped a number of friends with their weddings and adored each experience. It was like setting up a stage production and she'd gotten to be the director.

"That's great," Brett said, ready to press again. But before he could, a tall woman holding a clipboard came rushing through the door with Marc and what appeared to be the bride. The woman moved to the far wall, slid open a large paneled door and rustled through a storage area, emerging with a silk flower arrangement.

"We've got these that we can use for the tables," the woman said. Noting that the ensemble was somewhat weathered, she made an attempt to pretty it up. "I can get some extra people in here to fix them up a bit, but they're our standard stock for banquets. We've got plenty to fill the tables."

The bride, dressed in a simple veil and an expensive slip dress Rachel guessed was Vera Wang, studied the arrangement, her expression worried and less than enthused. "I guess they're better than nothing. You don't have any other colors?"

Looking nearly on the verge of tears, the bride crossed to the closet and peeked inside as Marc came over to greet Rachel and Brett.

"Sightseeing?" he asked.

"I was on my way back to my suite and had to stop." Rachel glanced around the room. "This is all so beautiful."

"Yeah, well, tell that to the bride. Her entire delivery of flowers just ended up in a pileup on Ten. We're scavenging around trying to see what we can do."

Rachel's heart sank. "The poor girl."

"What has Paige come up with?" Brett asked.

"We cleaned out the lobby boutique and managed to put together bouquets and boutonnières for the bridal party." He pointed to the arrangements the two women were hunkered over. "We've got these standbys for the tables that we keep around for banquets. It looks like Paige has sold her on those. But I guess she'd had some special rose trees ordered for the dance floor and stage setup. I don't know what we can do about that."

The woman circled the dance floor biting a fingernail she'd probably just had manicured. "We've got balloons," Paige offered. "We've got plenty of helium tanks, right, Marc?"

He and Brett stepped across the room and looked around. "Enough to do a decent job I'm sure."

"Balloons are tacky," the bride spat, tears threatening

to spill over into her hundred-dollar facial, ruining everything she'd probably spent half the day in the spa perfecting.

"We've got gold and silver—" Paige started.

"And if I come back for my anniversary, I'll remember that."

Paige eyed Marc as though the woman was incorrigible, which Rachel found inconsiderate. Had she never dreamed of the perfect wedding before? There were no do-overs when it came to weddings. A bride had only one shot at getting it right or the day would be gone forever. Who could blame her for being upset?

Stepping around the room, Rachel studied the area and listened while they brainstormed, none of their ideas apparently satisfying the bride. It sounded as though she was about to surrender the situation and accept what she had, when Rachel tossed out a thought.

"What about the potted topiaries on the plaza?" she called out.

The four turned to her and stared, their blank faces taking some of the wind out of what she thought might be a neat idea.

"You know. The ones around Desert Desserts and the coffee shop?" she went on. She made a gesture with her hands trying to describe the potted plants she'd remembered admiring.

Paige glared at Rachel as though she'd just spouted off something absurd, opened her mouth no doubt to say so, when the bride cut in.

"The ones in the cobalt-blue pots?"

"Yeah," Rachel said.

The bride looked alternately to Marc and Paige, her face brightening with hope. "Could we?"

Paige shook her head. "They're far too heavy and I'm certain they're full of bugs."

"Actually, we had to move them last month to reseal the sidewalk," Marc said. He glanced at Brett. "How long did it take Steve and Javier to move the whole lot?"

"It wasn't a big deal," Brett said. "And we stored them in the south banquet room for a week. I don't recall a problem with bugs."

"Too bad you couldn't decorate them with little white lights," Rachel started. "Wouldn't that be pretty?"

"Got about a million of those in the Christmas shed."

Marc looked at the gleeful expression on the bride's face. "It sounds like we have a plan?"

The bride nodded, bouncing on her heels before scattering about the room to decide how many they might need and where to put them. And with the two women busy, Marc glanced at Rachel, his eyes filled with pride and appreciation.

It touched a part of her she'd tried hard to shield, but she couldn't help it. *You did good,* the look said, nourishing a place in her that had been starved for a long time. She smiled to hide her fears, wishing that silly expression hadn't hit her as deeply as it did.

"I think we've got our solution," he said.

The bride went on babbling about the ornamental trees, all the while gushing over what a savior the resort was in helping her salvage her wedding. Marc called over to one of the maintenance workers then started barking orders into a walkie-talkie. And with the group suddenly in the throes of planning, Rachel took the opportunity to slip outside and head to her suite—because in spite of the fun of being the hero of the moment, she hadn't forgotten Brett and his inquisition.

He'd somehow caught on to them, and rather than stumble over denials and half truths, she decided she'd rather leave the man in the hands of his brother, letting Marc decide how much he should say.

12

IT WAS NEARLY SEVEN when Marc finally headed back to his office, having gotten the wedding off to a start and leaving it in the hands of Paige. Rachel's idea had saved the day, and Marc mused that if he had two people like her he could fire his whole management staff.

It was the latest in a number of revelations that had struck him lately, this one being how much Paige relied on him to solve problems she should be able to solve herself. No wonder he was buried each and every day. Between Brett's disinterest in the operations and Paige expecting Marc to run constant interference, he was carrying twice the load he'd expected when he started this venture.

Rachel wanted to know why he didn't relax more. Well, tonight she got a glimpse of the answer.

Welcome to Marc Strauss Crisis Management Service. Oh, and in my spare time I run a resort.

He crossed the lobby, thinking the only bright spots in his day had been the thanks from the Carlsons when they discovered their daughter's wedding was salvaged, and the same warm appreciation he'd gotten from Mrs. Lesnansky this morning. How ironic that both of them were owed to one beautiful brunette who was quickly finding a place next to his heart.

Reaching his office, he pulled open the door and found Brett sitting on his couch, his feet propped up on the coffee table and an unlit cigar between his teeth.

"Celebrating?" Marc asked.

Brett pulled the cigar from his mouth and twisted it between his fingers. "Just another day in paradise."

"I'm glad *you're* having a good time."

Marc shut the door behind him, walked over and collapsed at his desk, needing to get off his feet for the evening. Or maybe a month.

"Apparently, you are, too," Brett said. "When were you going to tell me you're sleeping with Rachel?"

Marc coughed. "What?"

"Come on. I know you are. I just want to know why you didn't tell me."

A dismal liar, Marc worked up a good laugh nonetheless. "That's ridiculous. What gave you such a harebrained idea?"

"Margaret noticed it first, but it got me thinking." Brett popped the cigar back into his mouth and spoke through his teeth. "You were awfully fun to dine with last night. In fact, I'd go as far as saying you were actually a likeable guy."

"So I crack a joke or two and you assume I'm getting laid? How long did it take you and Dr. Watson to put that together, Sherlock?"

"Twice in the past two weeks you turned down my offers to come over and watch a game."

He held up a hand. "You're right. Only a woman could keep me from my beloved Cubbies. Is that all you've got, Gil Grissom? Because I've got a date with a microwave tonight and I'd really like to get to it."

Brett laughed and pointed a finger at Marc. "Good one. And it's cute you're denying it and all, but you're too late. Rachel already spilled."

That wiped the smirk from Marc's face. "Rachel what?"

"She admitted it."

Marc closed his eyes and shook his head. "What did she do that for?" he muttered under his breath.

The cigar fell from Brett's mouth as his jaw hung agape. "You mean it's true?"

"You just said—"

"I was bluffing."

Marc shot out a curse and wondered if he still had enough strength on his brother to knock him into next Wednesday. Even if he didn't it might feel good trying.

"I can't believe this. You were so cocky when she first showed up. 'No special treatment. She's our ward, not a plaything,'" Brett said, mocking the words Marc knew all too well.

"So, crap happens."

"Apparently."

Marc pointed a finger at his brother. "This isn't something for you to spread around. The last thing I need is for this to leak to the press."

"Our lips are sealed. You don't have to worry about me and Margaret. But I'd say that dinners on the plaza probably aren't the greatest move."

"That was Rachel's idea, not mine, though I can't blame her really. She's literally spent every day and night cooped up in our hotel rooms trying to avoid the people and the press. She's going a little stir crazy. She hinted last night about getting out of here for a couple days, but I don't know how we'd pull that off. Here at the resort, we've got the excuse of the business relationship. Off the grounds? How would we explain that?"

"Take her up to Burton's cabin."

"Up to Miwok Lake?"

"It's beautiful up there. You've got the sun and the fresh air and there's not a soul within miles. I take dates up there all the time. It's a great place to get away from it all if you're looking for privacy."

Marc considered the idea, acknowledging it might not be a bad one. The Burtons were friends of the family who owned a cozy but nice cabin on a lake only a couple hours from the resort. On countless occasions, they'd told him and Brett it was theirs to use any time they wanted. Marc had never taken them up on it, though he'd always meant to.

"I was up there just a few months ago," Brett went on. "I don't remember seeing a soul once we passed the south fork. The water's been low these past couple years so they aren't getting the traffic they used to."

The more Marc considered, the more he liked the idea. Maybe a change of scenery was exactly what he needed. And for sure, he needed something. This relationship with Rachel was supposed to have been a quick fling, a release of sexual energy to temper an intense physical attraction brought on by too many months without a date. But that whole plan was falling apart, and the more time he spent with her, the more his mind started to wander to places it had no business going.

He wasn't supposed to be getting attached to Rachel, but here at the resort he was getting hit from every angle. Maybe getting out of this place would clear his perspective and help him see things straight.

At this point, with his heart running away from him and his inability to stop it, he was willing to give anything a try.

RACHEL GLANCED at Marc from the passenger seat of his BMW. "We've been driving for almost an hour. I think if someone were following us, you would have spotted them by now."

He checked the rearview mirror out of habit still needing to convince himself they'd managed to sneak out of the resort without anyone seeing them. After that fiasco with the press two weeks ago and now Brett and Margaret in the know, he couldn't take any more chances.

"You think so?"

"I know so. If any reporters had seen us leave, they'd be in the next lane snapping pictures right now."

He laughed, knowing she was right. He was simply being overly cautious, not wanting anything to spoil the weekend he'd planned. But at this stage of the game, he knew she was right and that it was time to relax and let their secret getaway begin.

"Okay, no more worries," he said. "Tell me more about your week. Rain's parents were sure taken with you. That was nice what you did for their family."

She shrugged. "It wasn't that big a deal. She was bored and I needed a girls' day out."

"Still, you made an impression, one that made a difference to their family."

"Yeah, well, we both know they'll all go back to old habits when they get home."

"Probably, but that's not the point. When my family went on vacation, we all went our separate ways the moment it was over. The folks went back to their jobs, me and Brett went back to our activities. That's how it works. But I still wouldn't change those times we had together. That's what vacations are about, connecting, even for just a little while."

Rachel didn't look convinced, but it was a concept Marc understood well. It was the whole reason he went into this profession, the kind of treatment he'd imagined for all his guests when he'd envisioned owning a resort. And after Rain's parents expressed their heartfelt thanks and went home yesterday, he'd asked himself when he'd ever taken the time to really pay attention to the guests he was supposedly hosting.

He hadn't missed the fact that in these few short weeks, Rachel had done the very thing he was still trying to grasp hold of. He hadn't gone into this field because he wanted to run a resort. He'd wanted to be a part of it, to team up with his staff and create an experience for his guests that went beyond a typical stay at a typical hotel. And while he'd spent three years trying to figure out how to do that, Rachel had waltzed in and showed him the way as if it was as simple as taking a breath.

"I suppose," she said, turning her face and staring wistfully out the window.

He reached out and took her hand in his. "You're a better person than you give yourself credit for, Rachel."

That got him a laugh. "I'm not the saint *you* think I am either."

He laughed with her. "Trust me. I don't think you're a saint. I wouldn't adore you so much if you were." Then he sobered his tone and squeezed her fingers. "I'm just wondering when you're going to stop torturing yourself and start believing in the real woman."

For a long time, she didn't respond. She simply

stared out the window as they made their way up the highway.

"I keep thinking about that poor maid," she finally said. "The one that landed me here. I wish I could do more to apologize, but the lawyers won't let me. If I could go back and do it all over again, things would go very differently."

"Then I think you should consider your stay here a success." When she turned and met his gaze, he added, "Seriously. You're not the spoiled princess I thought you were when you first showed up here. I was wrong. These past few weeks, you proved that tenfold."

That got her laughing again. "Only because you made me so angry I stormed off and sent Stefan away out of spite."

"And in the process, you discovered you didn't need him."

"He's pretty handy."

"He's annoying."

"I still can't make my way around my own computer."

"Half of America can't. I'm telling you, that man was suffocating you. I seriously hope that when you go back home, you'll stop relying on him so much."

His own comment darkened his mood. *Going back home to L.A.* The idea of that shouldn't bother him so much, but damned if it didn't.

Since high school, he'd had a plan for his life that didn't involve getting serious about a woman until he was ready. And up until now, he hadn't come close to considering it. The resort was burying him in responsibility. He still wasn't sure if even this brief overnight escapade would go uninterrupted by business. Trying to manage a serious relationship on top of everything else had disaster written all over it. And if he could keep his mind focused on that, he'd be fine.

"I am planning on making some changes when I get home," she said.

"You'd mentioned spending some time abroad."

She shook her head and sighed. "I don't know what I'll do. But after having this taste of a normal life, I only know that I don't want to go back to the way I'd been living. I'm done with reality shows and modeling and life in the public eye. I want to do something meaningful. I just don't know what."

A fleeting, irrational voice suggested he ask her not to go anywhere, to stay and help him run the resort. He knew without a doubt she'd be good at it, and he could definitely use the help. Then he tallied up all the reasons that idea was preposterous and clamped his mouth shut. He had to keep remembering that what he and Rachel had was sex. Really hot, great sex. And the more he kept his mind focused on that, the less chance he'd have of suggesting something they'd surely regret.

So as he turned off the highway and onto the last leg of their trip, he made himself a promise to keep his head about him and take their last week together in stride.

"A cabin on a lake," Rachel said, glancing at the scenery as they neared the south fork. "It sounds wonderful."

"It's very rustic."

"How rustic?"

"It has indoor plumbing and hot water."

"Then I'm sure it will be fine."

He drove through the wooded terrain beyond the more populated side of the lake where the water was deep for boating. He hadn't been here in years, yet already he was recalling how scenic and relaxing this place was. He wondered why he hadn't come up here more often. Rachel had been right. He did work too much, had let himself get too absorbed in the resort to the point where he hadn't so much as taken a day to revive his own spirit. The north side of the lake was quiet and serene, the water too shallow for any larger motorboats, which kept most of the people away. Surely, somewhere in the past three years he could have blown the dust off his fishing pole and spent the day up here.

But time had gotten away from him, and as they turned down the narrow drive that brought them to the cabin, he promised himself he wouldn't let time get away again.

"This is it?" she asked, looking at the modest A-frame structure perched a hundred yards from the water's edge.

"This is it."

He pulled the car up and parked, and she didn't waste time getting out and taking a look.

"This is lovely." She eyed him and frowned. "You made it sound like a shack."

"It's not Beverly Hills."

He found the hidden key and let them inside, moving first to open the large front window to air out the musty smell.

She followed him in and surveyed the space. The lake side of the cabin consisted of a large great room that opened to the kitchen. Above, a loft looked out over the lake and down to the dining area below. Two large suites took up the back, each with its own adjoining bath. And though the decor was made up of rustic plaids and knotty pine, everything was clean and new.

"You think I expect room service everywhere I go?" Rachel asked. "Aside from the dead fish on the wall, I think it's charming." She stepped over to the wide-mouth bass that eternally peered one eye over the dining-room table and touched a tentative finger to it. "Is it real?"

"Caught right out back, if I recall."

"Okay, then." She snapped her finger back and swiped it on her jeans as though it might have left behind scales.

Marc laughed, pulling her toward him and taking her in his arms. "If he bothers you, I can put him in the closet."

"I'm hardly intimidated by a bass."

"No, I suppose you're not."

She pressed a kiss to his lips. "Though if you plan on making love to me on this table, I'd rather not do it under the watchful eye of a fish."

He slid his hand around the nape of her neck and smoothed his mouth over hers, immediately feeling that heat that had become so familiar yet was still thrilling every time. Would he ever get enough of this? At what point would the sizzle fade to something he could more easily walk away from?

As he circled his arm around her waist and pulled her body close, he realized that might never happen. During these past couple weeks, the sizzle *had* faded. Gone was the thrilling spark in touching the forbidden fruit he'd spent too many days lusting over. In its place came the slow burn of something deeper and even more arousing. He hadn't wanted to acknowledge it. He'd chalked it up to infatuation, but with every day that passed, Rachel kept throwing more weight on his already burdened conscience.

Spending the day with Rain, helping Anita and her daughter get their book published, bringing gifts to the housekeeping staff, happily signing autographs and making friendly conversation with the very people whose curiosity perpetuates the current life she lives. Though the papers portray a spoiled, bungling rich girl, Marc had gotten close enough to see the real person. And what he found was a misunderstood woman who desperately wanted the world to love her.

It tugged at something he wasn't prepared to face.

Mingling his tongue with hers, he sank into the kiss and pushed his focus back where it belonged. He bathed in the luxury of her scent, the soft touch of her hair against his fingers, the luscious taste of her lips, her skin, her sex.

"There's a bedroom down the hall," he suggested.

He took her hand and led her toward the back of the cabin. Reorienting himself with the layout, he opted for the larger room on the west where a cross breeze freshened the air as he opened the two large windows. The light wind was cooled by the dense forest and scented with pine and earth. It brought back to him the memories of the restful time he spent here as a careless kid with few worries and even less responsibility. And as the surroundings soothed his spirit, he stripped his clothes and bared himself to the beautiful woman at his side.

She pulled her T-shirt over her head, revealing naked breasts that he wasted no time sampling. He took them in his palms, felt them against his lips and buried his face between them. She arched her body toward him, lacing her fingers into his hair and moaning soft words of encouragement.

"I love the way you touch me," she whispered.

He suckled a nipple. "I love the way you feel."

Lowering to his knees, he ran his tongue over her waist while he unfastened her jeans and slid them to the floor.

"This is what I'm looking for," he said through a groan, grabbing her ass and pressing kisses across her thighs and the sensitive space between. He took his time exploring, running his hands up and around her silky flesh as he used his mouth and tongue to build heat that rocked her to the balls of her feet.

Her throaty groans encouraged him, those slim fingers digging into his shoulders when he hit the right spot. She hissed when he slid a finger inside, smiled when he slid another, and when he touched his tongue to her clit he felt the weight of her body against him, the arousal snatching her grip against gravity.

Instead of taking her to the bed, he held her firm, his cock growing achingly hard as he sucked her toward orgasm like he'd learned to do so well. He loved this body, loved her responsiveness to his touch and his ability to coax it in any direction he chose. He licked her to the brink, then shied away, touching his lips to her thighs and toying his fingers around her core before coming in for another teasing pass. Her palms leaned heavy on his shoulders but she didn't make a move toward the bed, no doubt the sensations running through her too luxurious to deny for even a moment. So he worked her more quickly, sending her closer to that place that would break her apart.

He used his thumbs to part her folds, taking her fully in his mouth as she began to churn against him. Her breath heaved as her body swelled, her slick heat growing hotter, her fingers beginning to tremble with every light, fluttery stroke. And when she gasped and came hard, he lost himself in the glory of her surrender.

Right then, there was no existence outside this room. No troubling emotions, no conflicting desires to throw him off balance. When he and Rachel shut the world out and came together like this, all complications sifted down to two people enjoying the presence of each other, nothing less and nothing more.

But when he guided her to the bed and came to rest on top of her, he was hit with that same sensation he kept trying to deny. He could see it in her eyes, a connection further than skin deep. And he knew when she looked at him she could see it, too. No matter how much he didn't want this, no matter how many doubts and fears he had about this thing between them, Rachel was finding a way in, and he needed to hold on to his perspective before his heart got carried away.

He had to remember this life they'd led these past few weeks weren't reality. It was easy to get caught up in a fantasy when they'd shut themselves off from the world. Rachel had been his prisoner here, his private temptress owing only to him and his resort. She'd cut herself off from her friends and family, they'd kept the gawkers and the press from their own island of paradise.

Would this still seem so perfect when the real world came rushing back in?

A sharp wave of pleasure brushed the question from his mind, and he upped the tempo, sliding his hands over her sexy body and pressing soft kisses to her lips. Waves rushed over him, filling his body with ecstasy as the heat in Rachel's deep blue eyes warmed his heart. There was such beauty in those lips, the sweet curve of her jaw, the tender arch of her neck. He ran his fingers over those places, relishing the lazy smile he produced when he dipped his head and nipped her chin. But then the ripples grew to something dire, and he knew the climax was near.

Sliding his hand along her spine, he lifted her toward him and drove in harder, her breathy groans singing her satisfaction. He needed to get deeper, needed to hold her closer, and she seemed to understand when she wrapped her smooth legs around him and took him farther, pressing her mouth against his where she whispered an urgent, "Go."

It was all he could handle. White heat hit him squarely, taking her along with him, and he buried his head in the crook of her shoulder and cried out his release. His limbs came around hers, smoothing and stroking over bodies moving to the rhythm of climax. Lips crushed against lips, breath mingled with breath until, finally, they came to rest, the only sound the heavy beat of their hearts and the gentle coos of the forest outside.

And when he shifted onto the bed and spooned her against him, he felt grounded in the knowledge that he'd settled the battle between his head and his heart. Rachel offered him great sex and lots of it, something he hadn't enjoyed in far too long. That was all this was, and confusing that with something deeper would only lead to problems.

So as they rested and enjoyed the start of their weekend away, he promised himself that he'd keep his head about him, making sure that what he and Rachel shared stayed in the flesh where it belonged.

13

"I CAN DO THIS." Rachel dipped the oar into the water and used all her strength to paddle the canoe across the lake.

The boat lurched forward about three inches, nearly all of them lost when she swung the oar back for another stroke.

"I think we're moving forward," she said, forever the optimist.

Marc grinned and checked his watch. "At this rate, we should make it back to the cabin by...oh... September."

"You snot!"

He chuckled, bringing a reluctant smile to her face. Okay, so her first attempt at rowing a boat was pretty pathetic, but she deserved some points for giving it a try. She'd never been in a canoe before, and watching Marc paddle it around the lake looked so fun she wanted to know if she could do it.

It was something she never would have done a month ago, and she wondered, at what point had she stopped trying new things? When had she gotten so afraid of the scrutiny that she'd literally stopped living? No wonder she'd ended up so frustrated and angry. Somewhere along the line, she'd allowed the celebrity scene to suck away her free will, and only now, by really getting away from it all, was she finding her way back.

"If we accidentally drift ashore, we could get out and walk," he teased.

She gave him the evil eye. "Enough, already!"

Hoping to splash him, she slapped the oar hard against the water, but instead of sending a wave toward Marc, it came back on her instead, drenching her in murky lake water.

She screeched. "I can't believe I just did that."

As Marc laughed, she spat water from her lips and brushed a hand over her face. "Eww, gross. There's fish poop in this water, isn't there? I think I got some in my mouth."

Marc's laugh deepened to a roar, though in between hysterics, he had the decency to reach under the bench and toss her a hand towel.

Rachel searched for that familiar twinge of embarrassment, the heat of humility that always washed over her when she made a fool of herself, but it wasn't there. Instead, Marc's laughter sprouted giggles of her own and she gave in to the moment, chuckles bubbling from her chest even though she tried hard to tamp them down.

"If you tried that a hundred times, you'd never do it again," he cried, wiping tears from his eyes.

She brushed the towel over her face trying to stifle her laughter but it didn't work. It felt too good doing something silly and stupid without worrying about who was around snapping pictures or rolling their eyes. This was fun and free, an experience she hadn't enjoyed since her early years in high school. And the more she lived it, the more she didn't want to let it go.

"Are you ready to give me back the oar?" he asked.

"No, I'm going to learn how to row a canoe if it kills me."

"That's what I'm afraid of."

His resonant chuckles died down as she put the oar in the water and tried again, determined to master the art of maneuvering this sliver of a boat.

"You need to row faster," he said. "And don't put the oar so far into the water. That's what's making it so hard. You only need to brush the surface."

She did as he said and, lo and behold, the boat jutted forward twice as far with half the effort.

"There you go," he encouraged.

She paddled again and again, a bright smile spreading her lips as she propelled the boat across the water.

"This is fun!"

"You're doing great. Now paddle some on the other side so you don't start going in circles."

She kept rowing, taking them down through the dense inlet toward the open lake ahead. After spending last night enjoying the cabin and a romantic dinner under the stars, they'd gotten out early this morning to explore the lake. It was nearing noon and the sun was high. They'd been out here for a couple hours, basking in the scenery and the quiet of each other's company. Soon, they'd have to start packing up to head back to the resort, though if Rachel had her way, they'd never leave.

This life, both at the resort and here at the lake, was everything she'd ached for. One where she wasn't a celebrity, but a regular person, enjoying a real relationship with a man that was based on nothing more than respect, care and affection.

So many times she'd wanted to escape if she only knew where to go and what to do. And she knew she could. One good thing about the public was that they had short attention spans. Rachel knew all she had to do was disappear and eventually they'd lose interest and move on. She just hadn't known what to do with herself once she got up the nerve to walk away from everything she knew.

But now she was starting to form some ideas.

"Tell me about Paige," she asked.

Marc looked at her quizzically. "My event coordinator?"

"Is that what she is?"

A hint of sarcasm crossed his face. "That's debatable. Paige was one of the first people I hired. I liked her directness and she seemed sharp and efficient. She also came with good experience, but her credentials have been deteriorating. People don't like her. Half the staff won't work with her and she's made some enemies. I'm finding that I've got to run interference more and more these days." He gestured to Rachel. "Well, you got to see that for yourself night before last."

"Good to know it's not just me."

He laughed. "No, plenty of people share your reaction to Paige. Honestly, I don't know what I'm going to do about her."

She knew exactly what she wanted Marc to do with Paige. She wanted him to fire the woman so Rachel could take over the job herself. She wanted Marc to ask her to stay on, to continue exploring this relationship they'd started and see how far it could go.

If the old impulsive Rachel was still running the show, she might have spouted it all out right here and now, no doubt making a fool of herself in the process. Instead, she kept her mouth shut and silently wished she could figure out a way to make her old life go away and keep this new one she'd found instead.

"Why do you ask about Paige?" Marc asked.

"Just wondering how successful she was at her job. It looked fun. I was thinking about maybe trying to become a wedding planner."

"You'd be good at it, I'm sure."

"Really?" She wished that hadn't come out sounding as needy as it had.

"You're a good people person. I'm learning that's more important than I realized before. And you're creative, thinking on your toes like you did the other night, getting a quick feel for what the client wanted. You'd be a natural."

She smiled. "You think so?"

"I'm sure of it."

Then ask me to stay.

The words literally tumbled on her tongue and she had to bite her lip to keep from saying them. They'd only been together two weeks, had only known each other for three. If she blurted out the feelings in her heart he'd no doubt think her as crazy as the tabloids said. But she knew she wasn't. She'd been infatuated before, had thought she'd found Mr. Wonderful on more than one occasion. But none of that compared to what she had with Marc. These short weeks with him were like nothing she'd experienced before, and everything in her soul said this was something very special. She didn't want to walk away without seeing it through.

Her arms tired, she handed him back the oar and let him take over the rowing again, watching as he began paddling back to the dock. Those sinewy biceps contracted with each thrust, his upper body looking criminally delicious in his short-sleeved T-shirt. It wasn't

right that a man should be that sexy, getting her hot and
aroused doing nothing more than merely existing. How
was she supposed to keep her head about her? Right
now, she should be plotting a way to broach the subject
of their feelings for each other, maybe throwing out a
bone and seeing if he took it or kicked it aside. Instead,
she just wanted to slide her hands up under that shirt
and feel those firm muscles under her fingertips.

Slipping off her seat, she knelt before him and trailed
her hands up under the legs of his boxy cargo shorts.
His rowing came to an abrupt halt.

"Is it possible to have sex in a canoe?" she asked.

Though his expression was pure intrigue, he replied,
"I wouldn't recommend it, but we're only about fifteen
yards from the dock."

He thrust another long stroke of the oar through the
water as Rachel slipped her hands farther up the legs of
his shorts, gliding them along his firm thighs until her
fingers met his sharply growing erection.

"I don't think I can wait that long," she said.

Rising up on her knees, she nipped at his chin then
pressed her lips along his jaw, tasting his unique salty
essence that always rushed heat through her veins. He
brought a hand around her waist and she kissed him slow
and deep, savoring his familiar flavors as she stroked a
finger along his shaft. His breath hitched and he clasped
the back of her shirt, balling it in his hand as though he
were clinging to her for support—or maybe trying to
tear it off. She pulled her hands from under his shorts
and wrapped them around his waist, nudging closer,
sinking deeper, hoping he'd maybe rethink that idea of
having sex in a canoe on the lake.

She inched between his legs until her waist rested
against his cock, and he instinctively jutted forward, a

slow groan curling up his throat as she smoothed her hands up his back and twirled her tongue around his. She loved the earthy smells, the cool sound of water lashing against the boat, the distant caws of birds as they fluttered between the trees. And she loved it most with this heavenly body against her holding her close and teasing her with his tender lips and talented tongue.

For a long moment they kissed and kissed while Rachel slid her hands over his back and around his chest, and just when she thought they might find a way to take this further, Marc jerked and pulled away, letting out a curse as the oar slipped from his hand.

"Crap!" he yelled, quickly lurching out to grab it before it floated out of reach, but when he did, Rachel lost her balance and tumbled against the side of the boat.

It started a chain reaction that seemed to propel in slow motion, Marc grabbing the edge of the boat and attempting to shift back some balance, but it had come too late. The boat tipped too far and flipped over, sending Marc and Rachel cascading into the cold blue-green water.

She didn't even have time to yelp. As she treaded water, Marc grabbed the oar then held on to the boat. "Can you swim?" he asked.

"Yeah." She spat water from her mouth then brushed it from her eyes, turning to see that, fortunately, they were only a few yards from the shore.

He pushed the oar her way and she grabbed it. "Take this. I'll get the boat."

Then they made their way to the shore, her hands and feet squishing into the soppy bank as she got to the edge and found solid ground. When Marc came up behind her, she took one end of the canoe and helped pull it up to the grass where they dropped it in place and stood, their breath heavy and their bodies drenched.

"I told you sex in a canoe was a bad idea," he said, his eyes more teasing than scolding.

"You weren't exactly trying to stop me."

His mouth curved to a smile, bringing out that sexy dimple that always made her stomach flip. "When it comes to you, I maintain a definite disadvantage over my senses."

She looked down at her soaked body. "And now I'm going to have to take another shower."

"Damn."

Turning, she ran to the cabin, giggling as Marc came up behind her. On the deck, they tore off their clothes, Marc pulling his soppy wallet from his pants and bringing it inside, leaving everything else to dry out in the sun. Rachel stepped into the great room, ready to make a beeline to the shower when he slipped a hand around her waist and pulled her close.

"Where do you think you're going?" he asked.

He pecked a kiss to her lips.

"I'm covered with mucky fish poop water and my hair smells like algae. Where do you *think* I'm going?"

He cupped his hands to her bare butt and pulled her waist against him, and she noted the cold water hadn't tempered his erection.

"You're naked," he said. "Naked trumps lake water."

She wasn't going to argue with where this was going. Flipping open his wallet, he pulled out a condom and backed her toward the sofa. A grand idea, but she'd rather they had their fun in the shower with lots of sudsy soap and clean hot water.

"How about we—" She pointed down the hall.

"How about we finish what you started right here?" He pulled her down to the ground when they reached the large padded area rug that defined the space in the great room, coming to rest in front of the grand stone fireplace.

"But I—"

He came down on top of her. "I like you dirty. It's sexy. Besides," he said, palming her breast and sucking a nipple into his mouth, "that was a cruel thing you did back there. I think some sort of punishment is in order."

He bit her flesh and she yelped with delight, her body heating back up, every nip of his teeth making her forget that she wasn't cleaned and powdered like she'd always felt she should be. Once again, she found her inhibitions dissolving under the raw pleasure of this man and his talented body, and as he devoured her there on the floor, that familiar sad ache reared up in her chest.

This felt so wondrously right, the purity of their love-making, the simple luxury in their companionship, not to mention the ever-present passion his body evoked. He knew all the right places, had drummed up erogenous zones she hadn't realized she had, and never faltered in sending her past the limits of ecstasy.

With his hands and lips he tortured her body, building that glorious ache between her legs and draining her muscles of strength until they were limp strands of putty. He traced his fingers over her ribs then followed them with light kisses. Who knew that such a simple move could create such heat? It drove through her, leaving her hot and anxious and needy, begging for the heavy fill of his body inside hers.

He went down on her, rippling waves of pure pleasure pouring through her until she thought she would burst.

Her hands gripped against the carpet, fingers digging into the fuzzy strands while he pushed her to the edge then eased off, allowing the fierce sensation to ebb back to a slow burn.

How was she going to live without this? When next week came, how could she possibly pack up her things and walk away? She couldn't imagine it. This had become so much more than a casual affair. At least, it had to her.

"Come inside," she begged, gripping his shoulders and prodding him up where she cupped his face in her hands and touched her lips to his. "I want all of you," she whispered.

And while he obliged, she doubted he caught the true meaning behind her words.

Spreading her wide, he slipped his cock inside, letting out a long groan as he seated his body into hers. It felt so right, so perfect, and when he opened those blue-gray eyes and locked his gaze with hers, she knew these feelings weren't hers alone.

Gone was his playful glimmer she'd seen so many times. In its place was a look that sank straight to her heart. Need, want and affection spilled from those steely blues, the same one she'd been seeing over the past few days.

So many times, she'd told herself it was all in her imagination, her desire so strong that she was manifesting mutual feelings that probably didn't exist. But as she watched him watch her the doubt in her mind dissipated, pushed out with each stroke of his body in hers, of every brush of his finger against her cheek.

"You're amazing," he whispered, the power in those simple words pushing tears to the backs of her eyes. Not tears of joy or sadness, but tears of fear. Because when he uttered the words and pressed his lips to hers, she knew she'd fallen in love.

Emotions flooded through her, some giddy, some petrified. She wanted to hear those tender words of affection forever, from this man, in this spot, year after year until they both grew old and gray. She wanted to come to bed every night and have this strong body surround her, to rake away the struggles of the day and regenerate in each other's arms.

And as he thrust and stroked, sending them both to the edge and over, she knew this wasn't something she could pack up and walk away from. This was the life she'd searched for, the one she'd always wanted, and Marc was the man of her dreams. She had one week to figure it out, but somewhere in that time she'd come up with a plan. She wanted Marc and the things she'd found here, and before her time was up, she vowed to figure out a way to get it.

14

RACHEL STEPPED into her suite and shut the door behind her, tired from another day of maid work and feeling bittersweet about it being over. She only had three more days before her sentence was complete—good because she wasn't going to miss cleaning rooms. Bad because her time with Marc was running out and she still hadn't figured a way to broach the subject of their relationship.

A side of her kept hoping he would let her off the hook by bringing it up himself, but so far he hadn't said a word. And as the weekend neared she realized she would simply have to be blunt about it and throw the subject on the table.

She strolled over to the couch, kicked off her shoes and plopped down, picking up her cell phone and turning it on to see if any messages had come in during the day. She'd learned early on that Anita frowned on taking phone calls while they worked. It wasn't a hard and fast rule, but since they got to leave as soon as the rooms on her list were cleaned, wasting time with personal calls only made the day longer. So Rachel made a habit of leaving her cell phone behind when she showed up for duty.

Propping her feet on the table, she began checking for messages when the phone rang in her hand. It was Stefan.

She clicked it open. "Hello."

"Tell me it isn't true."

His voice had that dire sense of urgency she hadn't missed these past few weeks. Stefan had a habit of turning the mundane into national emergencies, and she rolled her eyes, acknowledging how calm her life had become without the constant dramatics.

"Tell you *what* isn't true?" she asked. "And hi, by the way. I'm good, thanks for asking. How are you?"

"Have you not seen the cover of the *National Star* today?"

"It's not on the top of my list of things to do, no."

The shrill in his voice kicked up a notch. "You mean you haven't spoken to your father?"

Her *father?* "Why would I talk to my dad?"

He huffed loudly. "Rachel, all hell's broken loose. Where have you been for the past three hours?"

"Working."

"Well, while you've been making beds, the press has been spreading the news that you're sleeping with Marc Strauss. They've even got a front-page picture of the two of you kissing on some balcony in the woods."

She jumped to her feet. "What?!"

"Even the mainstream media's picked up the story. Someone from the *Times* called your parole officer asking for a comment. They're questioning whether you've really been cleaning rooms up there, asking if they plan to investigate. It's a mess." He paused and took a breath. "I really don't need any more headaches right now. Tyler's threatening to take a job in Manhattan if I don't move in with him and start getting serious about our relationship. I've got deliveries that have gone missing, the imported tile I've waited months for is all wrong…"

Stefan's voice trailed from her consciousness as she tried to get a grip on the situation. The press found out about her and Marc? How could anyone have known? They'd been so careful. And she knew for a fact no one had followed them up to the cabin. How could anyone have come up with photos? They hadn't run into a soul.

She bit her lip and wracked her brain for answers. Had someone gotten wind of their plans? Was it possible Brett or Margaret had opened their mouths and told someone?

"Are you there?"

She blinked and absently answered, "Yeah."

"Rachel, you're scaring me. For God's sake, this isn't true, is it? These pictures are just doctored-up photos, right?"

"I…" She couldn't make the words come out of her mouth.

"Oh, heaven help me. It's true, isn't it? You're sleeping with Marc Strauss."

"That's…that's not anyone's business," she attempted, knowing what a waste of breath that statement was. Her life was *everyone's* business, like it or not.

The panic left Stefan's voice, replaced by a gravity that left her even more unsettled. "You need to call your father."

She tried to laugh it off. "It's a stupid tabloid smear. We don't have to grace it with a response."

"You aren't listening. Your parole officer is asking

questions. This isn't good, Rachel. You need to call Richard. He's been trying to get hold of you for over an hour now. Call him!"

"Fine." She disconnected the call and reluctantly dialed her father's number. Her fingers trembled and her heart hammered in her chest, though she didn't know why. She hadn't done anything wrong. So what if she and Marc were having an affair. That had nothing to do with the work she'd done here. And as the phone rang in her ear, she tried to drum up offense that people actually doubted that. It wasn't right. And what she did in her off hours wasn't anyone's business. But when she heard the click and her father's voice, her upper hand dissolved under the familiarity of the situation.

Another day, another screwup by Daddy's little girl.

"Rachel?"

"Hi, Dad. I just talked to Stefan."

His long exhale took the strength from her knees and she lowered to the couch.

"So you've heard. What do you have to say about this, Rachel?"

"I…" Her jaw bobbed, her throat tightening to the point where it was difficult to form words. "I haven't done anything wrong. My relationship with Marc is—"

"Oh, for chrissakes, Rachel. When are these kinds of antics going to end?"

She opened her mouth to defend herself then realized it was futile. What was he supposed to think? The day after he'd dropped her off at the resort she'd made a move on Marc, and her intentions hadn't been honorable. She'd pretty much spent the past ten years acting childish and irresponsible. How was he to know that she'd changed?

"Your parole officer is waiting for a statement, and when I tell her the truth, she'll send an investigator up there."

"I've done everything I'm supposed to do. Plenty of people will attest to that."

"I certainly hope so, or we've got another legal battle on our hands. They could throw you in jail."

"They won't."

He took a long breath and sighed. "I'm sending a car. Pack up and be ready to go."

"You can't! I've got three more days."

"Not now, you don't. We've got a mess to straighten out, and it starts with getting you out of that little love nest you've created up there."

She clenched her teeth and swallowed down the sting in that comment. It hurt to hear her father cheapen what she'd found with Marc, and it infuriated her to be spoken to like a child. But she knew a decade of foolish behavior wasn't going to be washed away overnight, and if she wanted to prove that she'd matured through this experience, throwing a tantrum wasn't the way to do it.

"Be ready to go this evening. The car will be there in a few hours."

"But—"

He clicked off the phone before she could say anything more, leaving her standing in her suite feeling as though her entire life had been taken from her. Old feelings of helplessness tried to take over, but she tamped them down, not willing to let even this setback throw her in a tailspin. This was only a bump in the road, a minor sidetrack in her pursuit of happiness. Besides, more important than her father and the court right now was getting to Marc before he found out about this on his own.

Tossing her cell phone on the couch, she headed for his office, using the walk to rehearse what she'd say when she found him. She had no idea how he'd respond to being thrown in the spotlight, and as she rushed across the grounds toward the main building, she realized that if they were to have a future together, he'd need to get used to publicity. It wasn't something she could make go away. She only hoped he had the temperament for it.

But when she reached his office and found him standing behind his desk, that hope was all but shattered. It only took one glimpse in those stormy gray eyes to see he'd already heard and that he wasn't taking it well.

Her eager steps slowed until her feet stopped moving altogether, held in place by fear as she searched his expression for something that might take her worries away.

"You heard," she uttered.

"I've been getting nonstop phone calls all afternoon."

And as if to underscore that statement, his phone rang again. Instead of answering it, he moved to close the door behind her.

She didn't like the stony expression on his face. It spoke of disgust and aggravation and, worst of all, regret. Marc was such a professional when it came to his job, she should have expected this. She only hoped she could do something to fix it.

"I'm sorry," she said.

He responded by pressing his lips into a line and moving back to his desk, and her heart sank at his lack of reassurance. So much for "No big deal," or, "It's not your fault." Everything about him said it *was* a big deal, and as for blame, well, that was still on the table.

"I don't understand. We were so careful. How could anyone have found out?" she asked, needing to keep the words flowing. The chill exuding from Marc threatened to freeze her up completely.

He smiled sourly. "I can tell you that much. It was Margaret, Brett's latest girlfriend. Apparently, she wasn't the ad executive she'd said she was."

"Margaret?!"

"Brett figured it out when he saw the photos at the cabin. She'd pressed him about where it was, then left the day after we got back. And just to be sure, he checked the credit card she used for the room. It belonged to one of the editors at the *National Star*."

A heavy wave of nausea and anger welled up her throat, but she worked to keep it in check.

"It's not the end of the world," Rachel assured him. "We haven't done anything wrong."

He looked at her as though she'd just made a joke. "It's a disaster, Rachel. I've got a board member freaking out over this, calling all the other board members and demanding my resignation."

"You can't be serious!"

The phone rang again and this time he snapped the button to send it to voice mail.

"This is *very* serious. They're claiming I acted unprofessionally, that I've jeopardized the reputation of the resort by creating this scandal. And the worst thing about it is I can't argue with a single accusation. I let attraction get the best of me and it's put the resort in a bad light. Phil Arnall is demanding I step down as a managing partner, and he's already got two more board members on the verge of agreeing with him."

"You can't possibly lose your job over this."

He shot her an angry look that pushed her back a step. "This is the real world, Rachel, where actions have consequences. Of course, I can lose my job over this." He clenched his teeth and spoke with a growl. "I don't own this place. I don't get to do what I want. If the board doesn't think I'm fit to manage their investment, they can toss me out." His face flushed and he stepped to the window, turning his back to her and fisting his hands at his sides. "I knew all of this. I told myself this a hundred times when you first showed up here. What I don't know is how I managed to forget it all."

She blinked. "So you're saying what happened between us was a mistake?"

"I should have been more responsible."

His dismissal hurt. So much so that she tried giving him another shot at coming up with a better answer, not ready to believe he was actually tossing away everything they'd shared. "You seriously regret getting involved with me?"

He didn't respond, and as she stood there waiting, all the happiness she'd gathered in the past three weeks slid away like sand through her fingers.

"I see," she said.

Her throat tightened and a flood of tears threatened to humiliate her. How could she have been so foolish? How could she have let this man become so important to her? And why—why—hadn't she seen it coming?

Hadn't she been through this enough times before? To every lover in her past she'd been either a play toy or a meal ticket. Why had she been so quick to think Marc was different?

"To think I thought I loved you," she muttered, wishing the words back the moment they spilled from her lips. She hadn't meant to say them out loud, and when Marc spun around and witnessed the pain in her eyes, she wished there was a hole in the ground where she could slip through and disappear.

"Rachel, I…" He stood there with his mouth agape, clearly not prepared to answer to that.

She shot up a quick hand. "Don't worry. I'm over it. *Way* over it."

Hot flames of embarrassment spread across her cheeks. Or was it anger? Most likely one feeding the other, because she was both humiliated for making a fool of herself and angry for letting it happen. She should have known better by now, should have never dropped her guard back when he was seducing her body and tempting her heart.

Straightening her shoulders, she jutted her chin and tried to hide her overwhelming urge to run and cower. "I'm sorry this happened. I'll talk to my father. I'm sure he can fix it so you don't lose your resort."

"I don't need your father's help."

"Why not? Why should you be different from the others? At least you score an extra point by only letting me fix what I screwed up in the first place."

"Stop it."

He took a step toward her but she backed away. The old bitter and angry Rachel Winston—the one she'd thought she'd buried forever—was quickly rearing up and taking over. And though she knew she was acting childish, she didn't care. It felt better than the shame and embarrassment it shrouded.

"Brett told me right from the start your only love was this resort," she said. "I should have listened. I can't believe I was dumb enough to think I might matter too."

Hot anger flared through his eyes. She'd apparently struck a nerve, and she didn't stop to analyze the satisfaction she got from that.

"Don't assume you know what matters to me," he snapped.

"Are you telling me I'm wrong?"

"You're not being fair. You have no idea how hard I've worked for this place."

"And you'd give anything to wipe out these past four weeks like they'd never happened. Right now you're standing there wishing like hell you'd never set eyes on me, aren't you?"

She stood there staring at him, wishing—*mentally begging*—him to say it wasn't true, that while he was angry and frustrated over the situation they were in, like her, he wouldn't trade this past month for anything in the world. Instead, he simply ground his teeth and stood there, his mind apparently processing a dozen answers, no doubt none of them good. And she wondered how her life had managed to go from total bliss to sheer hell in the matter of fifteen minutes.

An hour ago, she was happily plotting their evening, fantasizing about how life might be living on these grounds and working together. Now she realized the fantasy had been hers alone, and like so many other avenues she'd tried to explore, once again, when she turned down the final path there was nothing but a dead end sign at the end.

Except this time the loss was crushing, because this time she'd tasted something she'd really wanted with all her heart.

"Forget it," she said, backing toward the door until she clasped the handle. "I'm leaving tonight."

"Leaving?"

He hadn't expected to hear that, and for a fleeting second, she thought the news might have pushed him to express something—anything—that resembled the caring man she'd fallen in love with. But when she explained her father had sent a car, he only nodded in agreement.

"I suppose it's for the best," he said.

It cut the final slash through the only morsel of control she'd been holding on to, and before she burst into tears and came at him with both hands raised, she quickly turned the knob and opened the door behind her.

"Yeah, it's for the best," she quipped.

Then for the second time in four weeks, she rushed out of his office, beaten, broken and swearing off men for the rest of her life.

15

"WHY SO GLOOMY?" Brett asked, sidling up next to Marc as he stood under an archway and stared out over the lobby of the Clearwater Springs Resort.

The registration desk was busy this afternoon with a group of insurance agents checking in at the start of a four-day conference. It would be another hectic week, business as usual. One wouldn't even know that only last week this place had been crawling with press, all hell had broken loose, and Marc's job had been dangling by a thread.

Since then, the investigator from the San Diego courts had come and gone, certifying Rachel's sentence and closing the case without incident. And despite Phil Arnall's best efforts, the board members sided against him, agreeing to keep Marc on as managing partner and basically telling Phil to go blow his horn somewhere else. In the blink of an eye all of Marc's problems had disappeared and life had gone back to normal.

Except that he didn't feel anything close to normal.

"Everything blew over just like I said it would," Brett went on. "So how come even though you say you forgive me for Margaret I keep getting the feeling you haven't?"

Marc shoved his hands in his pockets and kept observing the activity. "I told you it's over and forgotten."

Brett eyed him, too smart to have missed all the falsities in that statement, but nonetheless he didn't press. They both knew that when it came to the matter of Rachel Winston, it was neither over nor forgotten.

So many times since she left the resort last week, Marc had wished he could wind the clock back and do it all over. Though unlike Rachel believed, he didn't want to do over the past month entirely. He only wanted to step back to that moment she came into his office after their affair had hit the press and he'd acted heartless and cold. It brought a pain to his gut every time he replayed their conversation in his mind. He doubted the look of devastation in Rachel's eyes would ever leave him completely.

He'd called her the very next day, trying to apologize and explain that he'd been angry with his situation and had shamelessly taken his frustrations out on her. He'd hated that his career and everything he'd worked for all these years still wasn't his, that his life wasn't his own, and that despite the tiring hours he put into managing this resort, he still had to answer to people like Phil Arnall. He'd been infuriated by the inquisition and had taken it out on the easiest target, tearing Rachel's feelings apart with his inability to acknowledge what was really in his heart.

And when he'd called her up to say all that, she'd only told him what he could do with his apologies, throwing out a couple more suggestions which were technically anatomically impossible, before hanging up in his ear.

She wasn't having anything to do with him, and

though he couldn't blame her, he also couldn't accept the idea that there was nothing he could do to make things right again. He had to make things right again. Because he'd learned during this past week that though he had his life back again, none of it seemed to matter without her by his side.

"I talked to Rachel yesterday," Brett said, as though he'd read Marc's thoughts.

Marc shot a glance to his brother. "And?"

Brett's look was apologetic. "Her mom has convinced her to spend some time in Italy with her."

The pain in Marc's gut swelled.

"She's leaving the country?"

"Not right away. She's still got a few days of her sentence to deal with. They're working on the arrangements for that, but when she's done, she'll be taking off for a few months. I guess Abigail bought a vacation home out there and she wants Rachel to help decorate it."

Brett might as well have said she was traveling to Mars, the feeling of permanence in that move deepening the troubled thoughts that had haunted him all week.

Why hadn't he stopped her from leaving when he had the chance? Or at the very least, why hadn't he had the self-awareness to admit that he hadn't been in a position to discuss their relationship when she'd stormed into his office? Her timing had been horrible. He'd been inundated with threats by Phil and concerned calls by the board, and every news media outlet in California had been harassing him for quotes. She'd caught him in the throes of shock, fear and anger, and though he'd tried to shut his mouth and keep from saying something he'd regret, in the end it was what he *hadn't* said that had done the most damage.

Regardless, he needed to find a way to fix this, to

settle the turbulence that had taken over his conscience
the moment he'd met Rachel Winston. He needed clarity.
And most of all, he needed to understand why, as he
stood in this lobby and surveyed everything he'd worked
so hard to accomplish, not a stitch of it mattered to him
anymore.

The walkie-talkie on his belt sounded with the crack-
ling voice of Kyle in maintenance, no doubt needing a
management decision on something involving the conference. But instead of answering it, he handed it to
Brett.

"Handle this."

Brett stared at the device as if it was kryptonite.
"What are you talking about?"

Reaching out and grabbing Brett's wrist, he placed it
in his hand. "Kyle needs something. I'm busy. You take
it."

"It's a conference. I don't do—"

"You do now."

Then Marc took out his pager and cell phone and
handed those to Brett, as well. "I'm taking the afternoon
off. You're officially in charge."

"What am I supposed to do?"

Marc started walking toward the front lobby doors,
tossing over his shoulder, "You'll figure it out."

And with Brett stuttering objections, Marc pulled off
his suit jacket, threw it on a nearby chair and stepped
through the double glass doors into the hot afternoon.

Warm air spilled over him as he walked the length of
the carport, stopping at the edge of the shaded terrace
and taking a moment to contemplate where he wanted
to go. He rolled up his sleeves as he watched the airport
shuttles and taxis pull up to the drive and drop off car-
loads of business travelers coming in for the conference.

He stood on the sidelines observing them, reminding himself that when he was young and dreaming about running a resort, those dreams hadn't involved catering to large corporate functions. Events like these were a lot of work and they offered little reward other than financial profit. But Marc hadn't gone into this business to become a rich man. He'd wanted to connect with people, to bring families together and help them make the most of the time they spent together. Staring out over the bustle of arrivals, no doubt many of them were here to get *away* from their families. Yet Marc would still be spending the next four days working twelve-hour shifts to accommodate them.

He sighed and crossed the grounds, walking down the stone pathway around the main building toward the suites and the plaza beyond. Was this really everything he'd ever wanted?

He reflected on the times Rachel had insinuated that it wasn't. It was one of the reasons he'd been both intrigued by her yet put off at the same time. She had an ability to see straight through him, to cut straight to the conflict in his life and note all the places where his carefully laid-out plans didn't jibe with the life he said he'd wanted. And instead of being open to what she'd said, he'd shut it out, too stubborn and bullheaded to consider the thought that somewhere in the pursuit of his dreams he might have gotten it all wrong.

He passed one of the four swimming pools on the grounds. This particular pool was set up like an island lagoon, edged with large boulders and waterfalls and surrounded by palms. Miguel ran the poolside bar here, and though Marc knew the man well, he couldn't remember the last time he'd actually sat and enjoyed a drink. He recalled the time he'd first set eyes on this spot, thinking how great it would be to stand on one of those boulders and dive into the cool water on a hot day.

He'd never done it once.

Crossing to the plaza, he stopped to really look at what he'd built here over the past three years. He'd spent so many years working for this, tirelessly calling in every favor he could, squeezing out every connection he'd ever made to pull together the partnership to buy Clearwater Springs. A huge chunk of his life was here in these stones, poured into this earth and etched into the bricks and tiles and wood he'd so carefully restored.

Could he actually consider walking away from it all?

A month ago a thought like that would have been dismissed as ludicrous. In fact, he would have laughed it off as absurd right up to a week ago when he thought he'd lost it all. But when the dust had settled and he'd stopped being ruled by his fears, he realized he wanted Rachel more than he wanted this resort. And he didn't just want her back here with him. He wanted her with him sharing a life that offered something even more.

Stepping over to one of the refreshment carts, he bought a bottle of water and took a seat on a bench next to an elderly gentleman who was sitting alone in the shade.

"Enjoying your stay?" he asked the man, needing a distraction, if only momentarily.

The old man nodded. "Yes, yes. It's a very nice place."

Marc held out a hand. "I'm Marc Strauss. I run the resort."

The man smiled and accepted it. "Hank Short."

"You here with family?"

Hank repositioned his long frame, crossing his legs and throwing an arm over the back of the bench so that he was facing Marc. "My granddaughter wants to get married here. She's brought the whole crew. I think it's a reconnaissance mission to get us all to pay for it. Both she and my daughter have been working me and the wife since they announced the engagement."

Marc chuckled. "If they get their way, we'll make sure to make it worth your money."

Hank grinned, his friendly brown eyes and wide mouth bringing a smile to Marc's face and easing some of the heaviness in his chest.

"I don't doubt that," Hank said. "This is a beautiful spot of land here."

"We work hard on it."

The two made casual conversation as they rested in the shade. Apparently, most of Hank's family had gone off with one of Paige's assistants to discuss the various options Clearwater Springs offered for hosting weddings. And while Hank's family busied themselves with the details, he'd opted to spend the afternoon relaxing on the plaza.

"I spent forty years on my feet," Hank said. "Now, I only get up when I absolutely have to."

Marc laughed. "What did you do on your feet for forty years?"

"I was a supply sergeant for the army until '57. Then I spent the next thirty years as a doorman for the Beverly Hills Hilton."

"No kidding."

Marc listened intently as Hank told stories of his years with the Hilton, keeping Marc rapt with tales of Hank's experiences there and the people he'd come across, from celebrities to politicians to mobsters. The man had led a fascinating life, and Marc so enjoyed the tales that he hadn't realized an hour had gone by before Hank's family tracked him down.

They stood and made introductions, and Marc shook the hands of Hank's family and chatted with them for a few moments. And when they took off for dinner, Marc sat down and came face-to-face with what it was that had been wrong with his equation. This was the one piece of the puzzle he hadn't factored when he was putting together his prospectus, wooing investors and slaving to get this resort on the map. The intangible part of his dream that he hadn't been able to put on paper, but that Rachel had seen so clearly.

Time.

Time and freedom and independence. The ability to do what he wanted, when he wanted, instead of being chained to the job and a foreman for a board who only cared about the bottom line.

He thought back to all the things Rachel had said to him over the weeks that she'd been here, starting with that very first time they'd made love in her bed. He'd shared with her his dreams, talked about his goals and what he'd set out to accomplish, and each time she'd looked at him quizzically as if she couldn't reconcile what he was saying with what he was doing here at Clearwater Springs.

Now, he understood that quizzical look completely. He understood all of it from his feelings for her to the missing link in his plans that controlled the power to take a good life and make it great.

So there, under the shade of the palm trees, Marc stared out over everything he'd built and came up with a new plan.

While he couldn't change the past and the hurtful

way he'd treated Rachel, he could change the future. And if he played his cards right, he might be able to talk her into giving him another chance, and in the process, offer her something even better than the short slice of paradise they'd shared here together.

16

RACHEL STEPPED FROM her closet into her bedroom and held up a cashmere sweater. "I forgot to ask my mom what the weather is like in Italy. Do you think I'll need sweaters?"

Her friend Pamela was spread across the couch thumbing through the latest *Vogue* magazine. "Honestly, I don't know why you're packing any clothes at all. You're going to *Italy*. Pack an overnight bag with the essentials then buy all new when you get there." She pointed her French manicured fingernail toward Rachel's sweater. "That's cute, but *so* California. Why would you want to drag it to one of the fashion capitals of the world? That's like showing up at Wolfgang Puck's with a bag of Oreos."

Rachel turned her eyes to Stefan, who was sitting at her desk clicking away at her laptop.

"Want me to look up the weather forecast?" he asked.

"No, that's all right."

She returned the sweater to her closet, thinking about what Pamela had said and trying to drum up excitement for the trip. Instead, she only wished she was back in

Palm Springs, living the last week over again but this time getting it right.

Once again, she'd taken something good and royally screwed it up beyond repair. Yes, she'd been hurt and angry when she'd left Marc's office. And, yes, she'd had every right to be upset with the way he'd reacted when their affair had hit the tabloids. But as was typical of her when things didn't go her way, she couldn't simply let a bad situation be, she had to blow it up into bits until there was nothing left to salvage.

Marc had called up and so sweetly tried to apologize, and what did she do but tear the man to shreds and slam the phone in his ear. He'd hurt her and she'd taken her opportunity to hurt him back. Hip-hip hooray for that little victory.

Except she was tired of the childish behavior and disgusted with the fact that she hadn't matured as much as she thought she had these past few months. She really thought she'd gone beyond the foolish antics that had caused her so much trouble in the past. Apparently, she still had a lot of growing up to do.

Pulling two of her favorite skirts from her closet, she stepped back into the bedroom to pack them, telling herself that it didn't matter. Marc had only called to apologize for the way they'd left things. He hadn't called to profess his undying love for her, and he certainly wasn't on the phone to beg her to come back. It was time to face the fact that they were both too messed up for a relationship—two people perfect for each other who unfortunately met at the wrong time in their lives. Marc wasn't going to let a woman in until he'd secured his dream career, and she wouldn't manage to keep a relationship until she learned to stop acting like a spoiled child every time she didn't get her way.

"Oh, my God, would you cheer up?" Pamela spouted. "It's nearly storming in here with that big cloud of gloom over your head. You're going to Italy! You'll be spending a month with your mother. When was the last time you two had some girl time together?"

"She has a new Italian boyfriend, apparently," Rachel said, knowing better than to expect a lot of attention from her mother when she showed up in Milan. To Abigail, Rachel was an accessory. Always would be. In all honesty, the only reason Rachel was making the trip was to get as far away from Marc as she could, hoping maybe the distance and the change of scenery would help take him off her mind.

"That's what *you* need. An Italian fling. I hear the men over there are way less sexually repressed than they are in the States."

Stefan raised a hand. "I'll vouch for that. I dated an Italian one time. The guy was an animal."

Pamela set down her magazine. "There you go. A hot Italian man to go with that fiery personality of yours."

"Ha! We'd kill each other," Rachel blurted.

"He'd be perfect for you."

"*Marc* was perfect for me."

Crap, she hadn't meant to say that out loud. She'd already spent two weeks crying on her friend's shoulder. Pamela was beginning to lose patience, as noted by the glance she and Stefan shared.

"What?" Rachel asked, eyeing the two.

Stefan threw up his hands. "I'm not saying another word. You already know how I feel about *Strauss the Louse*."

Rachel frowned.

"Oh, c'mon, Rach," Pamela said. "The guy's a hotel manager. You can do so much better."

"You're dating a bartender."

"Only until he lands his first big movie deal. Then he'll be a world-famous actor."

With the help of Pamela's father, an award-winning director, no doubt.

Rachel shook her head and retreated to her closet. Yes, she hated this life, even more so now that she'd had a taste of something different. Everyone around her was shallow, self-centered and out for some sort of personal gain, up to and including her two closest friends right here in this room. Of course, they weren't like that intentionally and certainly wouldn't see those qualities within themselves. Pamela would never admit that her latest boyfriend was only using her for the connections, and in the end it wouldn't matter. No doubt, Pamela would get bored with him first and move on to something new. It was just the Hollywood way, where everyone played the game and ran with it or got out.

And at this point, Rachel knew for sure she couldn't play the game anymore. She wanted out, and if she couldn't escape to Palm Springs, she'd have to take off to Italy and figure out where to go from there.

But Pamela had a point. Leaving town with her spirits down and her attitude in the gutter wouldn't make for a fresh start. She needed to get excited about this trip, to start appreciating the positives like the fact that the legal battles she'd been dealing with for the past six months were finally over. She'd also severed all her commitments with her agent and the modeling firm that had employed her over the past several years. She had nothing outstanding, only a clean slate and plenty of free time. She should be looking at this as a time of renewal instead of moaning over what she'd lost.

The power of positive thinking. Accept what you can't control and make a plan for what you can.

She'd repeated those lines to herself countless times. Now it was time to really live it.

"Oh...my...God!" Stefan cried, causing Rachel to rush to the doorway of her closet.

"Gossip-bits.com is speculating that you're pregnant." His eyes were wide as he stared at her computer screen.

Pamela shot out a laugh. "Can I name the baby?"

Rachel only rolled her eyes. "I told you that if you insist on scouring the Internet I don't want to hear anything about what you find."

"Do you know how this rumor will take off once everyone gets wind that you've gone abroad? They'll be convinced you've gone away to have a secret baby."

"It isn't 1960 anymore. Women don't run off to have secret babies, especially not in Hollywood. The bump is practically a fashion statement right now."

"You know why this is happening," Stefan scolded. "You refuse to give anyone an interview or make the slightest comment about your time at Clearwater Springs. It's not like you, so everyone's imaginations are running wild. Every magazine and celebrity news show is dying to get you to talk. If you'd just set the record straight, everyone would take a chill pill."

It was a lie and Rachel knew it. Stefan was only prodding her because he lived off the drama she'd always provided, and she wondered how he would manage once he got a real dose of her new life and how she intended to live it. Like it or not, he'd have to get used to the new Rachel Winston.

"I told you already, that's out of the question. I'm done with interviews, appearances and statements to the press." She folded a few T-shirts and set them in her suitcase. "Let them speculate all they want. I'm done talking to those vultures, and I'm *especially* not talking to them about Marc." Then she added under her breath, "Besides, it's still too fresh."

"Rach, if you're that crazy about the guy, go see him," Pamela urged. "You've been moping around for two weeks. I'm seriously considering dumping you as my BFF. This whole downer thing is getting on my nerves."

"Actually, I am. When I get back from Italy, I plan to visit the resort. I've got a number of people there I never properly said my goodbyes to, and I'm hoping by that time, I can come back without causing a media uproar."

And maybe by that time, she'd be able to look Marc in the eye, express her regret for the way she'd spoken to him and finally put their affair to rest without hard feelings on either side. She knew she'd never feel right until she made her peace there, but right now wasn't the time. She needed Italy, a change in scenery, a cleansing of the spirit, so to speak, before she could face the unfinished business she'd left behind.

At least, for now, that was her plan.

Her housekeeper, Annette, came to the door. "Ms. Winston, the limo is here."

Rachel checked her watch. "I'm sorry, I lost track of time. I'll be ready in just a moment."

Annette nodded and left, and Rachel rushed to finish her packing while both Pamela and Stefan gathered their things and said their goodbyes.

"Like I said, if I can get away I'll fly out and see how you're doing," Pamela said, pressing an air kiss toward Rachel's left cheek.

Rachel smiled. "I'd like that."

"You're to call me when you get there," Stefan insisted.

"I will." She gave them both hugs and sent them on their way, wrapping up the last of her packing while the chauffeur took her bags to the car.

Stepping down the stairs and out to the driveway, she noted the stretch limousine her father arranged. Had that really been necessary? Easily, she could have managed with just a car, but she smiled when she realized it was probably his way of trying to cheer her up. Despite all the faults in their relationship, he truly was the one man who would always stick by her no matter how badly she messed up her life, and for that, she'd always appreciate him.

The driver opened the back door and she slipped inside, raising a brow when she noted not only the fully stocked bar, but some sort of lunch on ice. When she had dinner with her dad two nights ago, he'd noted she'd lost some weight. No doubt, the covered plates contained something to put meat on her bones, but admittedly, she hadn't had much of an appetite lately. It was something she intended to remedy when she got to Milan.

"Can I mix you a drink before we go?" the driver asked.

She shook her head and settled into the seat.

"If there's anything you need, you can reach me through the intercom," he said, before shutting the door and leaving her within the quiet of the large dimly lit space.

With the windows tinted and privacy screen up, it was like a room fit for meditation, and as the limo pulled away from the driveway, she kicked off her sandals, closed her eyes and started the deep breathing exercises she'd learned from a relaxation therapist. With every breath she took, she visualized exhaling the bits of her past, regrets, embarrassments and unspoken apologies. She sucked in clean air then breathed out more, letting go of the things that left her feeling sad and depressed and opening mental windows for fresh new experiences to come through.

For over a half hour, she relaxed to the smooth rocking of the moving car, listening to the faint noises of the freeway and letting the calm quiet of the space soothe her tired spirit. And after a while, she'd managed to get herself so relaxed she'd nearly slipped off into sleep.

But then the limo hit a bump and she happened to glance out the window to see a passing highway sign. She blinked. Not certain she'd seen it correctly she turned and looked out the back window. *What the heck?*

She hit the button to the intercom. "Excuse me, but we're supposed to be going to LAX."

"The airport?" the driver asked.

"Yes. You're going the wrong way."

Great. She only hoped they'd left early enough so that she wouldn't miss her flight.

"According to Mr. Winston, there's been a change of plans," the man said.

"What do you mean a change of plans? I've got a plane to catch. Where are you taking me?"

Instead of answering her question, the intercom clicked off and the privacy screen began to roll down. And when it did, Rachel realized that there were two men in the front seat, the driver and—

He turned around and smiled, hitting her with that big, gorgeous one-two punch that always made her fluttery inside and turned her legs to jelly.

Marc!

"Sorry, babe," he said, grinning from the front seat. "You're not going to Italy. You're coming with me."

17

THE LIMOUSINE STOPPED briefly at the side of the road and Marc moved from the front seat to the back, restoring the privacy screen and shutting off the intercom as the driver took off to a destination Rachel could only hope for.

"What's going on?" she asked, her voice faint from the air that couldn't manage to move from her lungs.

She was afraid to breathe—afraid to blink—for fear that this was all some sort of dream. Maybe that relaxation technique had worked better than she thought. She'd nodded off into a deep sleep and all of this was about to vanish into a cloud of disappointment when she woke up and discovered none of it was real.

But when Marc scooted next to her, cupped her face and pressed his warm lips to hers, she knew she never could have slept through the swarm of tingles in her stomach.

This was real.

He was here.

And he was kissing her as if everything in the world was right and perfect between them.

Not asking questions, she gripped a hand to his

button-down dress shirt and pulled him close, breathing deeply, melding her tongue with his to soak in everything she'd missed so badly. His scent, his taste, the firm feel of his chest against her fingers, the soft touch of his hair, the rough shave of his chin. She took it all in with hungry greed, not wondering why he was here or what his plans were, but just aching for this to last.

He moaned and clutched her waist, whispering to her lips words of affection.

"I've missed you," he uttered between kisses.

New life boiled through her veins and her heartbeat sped, every stroke of his hands over her body, every eager lap of his tongue, every brush of his lips pulsing warmth through her until she thought she might ignite. And though her thirst for his touch was so dire, questions wouldn't stop nibbling at her heels, not to mention the feelings she needed to express.

Pulling away, she touched his chin and whispered, "I'm so sorry. I was so—"

He held a finger to her lips. "Don't. We both have things to apologize for. Not now." Then he yanked her shirt from the waist of her skirt and slipped his hands up under the fabric, touching hot skin to hot skin. "The only thing that needs to be said right now is that I let you get away, and that was a mistake that I'm correcting right now."

Squaring those sparkling blue-gray eyes with hers, he studied her closely. "Just tell me you'll come back."

Her smile spread so wide she felt it stretch all the way to her ears. "I don't want to be anywhere else."

He moved off the leather seat and knelt between her legs, pulling her shirt up over her head then going to work on her bra. As he shed the fabric, she unbuttoned his shirt and spread it open, working to lose the barriers so they could come together flesh to flesh.

His breath was hot against her skin as he kissed a path from the sensitive spot under her ear all the way down to her bare breasts. He did it with speed, but it still felt achingly slow. It had only been two weeks since they'd connected like this, but it seemed like a lifetime. She'd felt lone and hollow without him. Now every slip of his tongue poured a new sense of desire through her, watering her spirit like a wilted flower perking up and reaching toward the sun. She hadn't thought she'd feel this way again, had thought she'd lost this bone-melting sensation forever. And now that it was back, she wanted all of it and fast.

As he cupped her breasts and feasted, she reached back and unfastened her skirt, tugging the clothing off her hips until she was bare and exposed for him. It was then that he stopped and studied her, eyeing her body and tracing his gaze with appreciating fingers.

"You're the most beautiful creature I've ever seen," he whispered. Then he bent between her legs and pressed his lips to her inner thigh.

A sharp swirl of tingles sped over her then circled between her legs, bringing a quick pulse to her sex and curling the tips of her toes.

"I've missed this," he said, nibbling his way toward the apex. "I've missed all of you." And when he brushed his tongue over her clit, she nearly came apart right then.

"Ohhh," he groaned. Then he did it again, and this time the long stroke sucked the air from her chest.

She grabbed onto his shirt and coaxed his mouth up to hers, not wanting to lose herself like this. She wanted his body inside hers, pushing her to the brink while sinking into those steely blue eyes and searching for answers to all the questions that swarmed around her.

She kissed him deeply and unfastened his belt. "Make love to me," she urged, and he wasted no time in pulling condoms from his pocket and tossing off his slacks.

His cock was hard and ready, telling her he'd ached for this as much as she had. And while he sheathed himself, she scooted to the edge of the seat and opened herself to him.

Slow and smoothly, he slipped inside, restoring her spirit as he filled her. She curved her back to receive him, a warm wave of calm washing over her when he'd gone all the way and his firm hips came to rest against her thighs. And for a long time, he stayed there, holding her face in his hands and staring into her eyes.

"I love you, Rachel." He searched her expression as tears swept up from somewhere deep in her chest. "You said you thought you'd loved me. Was that true?"

The faint curve of his mouth said he already had the answer, but she offered it anyway.

"I never thought. I always knew."

That curve turned into a full gleaming smile. "I've got an offer for you, but first you need to know how much you mean to me. And not just like this." He thrust inside her again, sending another wave over her that sped straight up her spine.

"I'm getting the picture," she said, her voice weak as she fought through a wall of thrill, disbelief and physical pleasure.

He kissed her gently. "I want you back again. And this time, I want you for good."

"I'd love that." She squirmed under the pressure of his erection, the gentle rocking of the limo brushing the base of his shaft against her clit and pushing her close to orgasm even if he hadn't intended it. "But right now you need to—ohhh."

He stroked and stroked, starting a rhythm that she could hardly bear. Her legs trembled as she tried to hold on, to wait for his climax to peak and join with hers, but it was all too much. This surprise reunion, his profession of love and his plans for their future, not to mention the smooth feel of his hard naked body against hers. It all came together to overpower her will, and as he moved and thrust, she exploded into a sea of wet heat and glorious joy.

The orgasm took quick control, her muscles fisting and pulsing, her hips jerking and her breath reducing to light whispers. It turned the playful warmth in Marc's eyes to something urgent, and just as the warm blanket of velvet smoothed over her, his gaze clouded over and he lost himself inside her.

He carried her own release beyond the edge, grunting and yanking her up off the seat and onto his lap, her body impaled on his as he spilled and bucked and came. They wrapped their arms around each other and held on tight, his teeth digging into her shoulder while she cupped his head and held him close. She pumped and thrust, drawing out everything he had to offer, while she basked in the feel of his body joined with hers, his bare chest heaving against her breasts, the light glistening of sweat shimmering over them as the orgasm peaked and then finally calmed.

And when it was over, they stayed there for a long time, holding each other, kissing and caressing, neither daring to be the first to break the connection they'd restored.

He brushed his hand across her cheek and laced his

fingers through her hair, turning his lips to her ear and whispering, "I love you."

The words tightened her throat, and she studied his eyes. "You really mean that."

"Yes."

"I love you, too. I've been so miserable. I'm so sorry for the way I acted."

"I deserved it."

She tried to object, but he covered her mouth with his and sank in for a long, luxurious kiss. Then he smiled and said, "You and I, we're right together. We keep each other real, Rachel. I think that's a good thing. And don't be mistaken. If you do something that warrants an apology, I'll demand it. But this time, I was the fool who dismissed everything we shared and let you walk out without so much as a goodbye. I deserved everything I got."

"But I can have a temper sometimes."

He grinned. "Perfect. I've got a thick skull. An occasional jackhammer is exactly what I need."

She giggled and began to choke up. None of this seemed real. Any moment, she feared the car would stop, the door would open and a big group of people would stand up and cheer, "You've been punk'd!"

But there was nothing mistaking that look in Marc's eyes, and it was there that she saw this *was* real, he really did love her, and the future she'd been so afraid to dream of was actually coming true.

"So we're going back to Clearwater Springs?" she asked.

"Not exactly." He lifted her up to the seat. "That's part of the proposition I have for you."

Instead of explaining, he grabbed her clothes and handed them to her then got dressed himself, and when they'd both settled back in their seats, he pointed to the two plates that had been sitting on ice.

"Did you take a peek at those?"

She shook her head. "I assumed it was lunch."

He smiled. "It's our future."

He raised the lid from the first plate to reveal a mound of ripe plump strawberries with long stems. Taking one in his hand, he put an arm around her and held it between them. "This was the life you gave me back at Clearwater Springs, remember?" He brushed the berry over her lips and encouraged her to take a bite. "How did you say it? Sweet, a little tangy, loaded with flavor and color."

It tasted delicious, ripe and juicy, but instead of offering her the rest, he ate the last of it himself then nodded in agreement.

"I would consider that a very satisfying life," he said. "But you got me thinking about what I'd been doing with my career and whether or not I'd achieved the life I'd really wanted. Like I said, we keep each other real. And I realized that while this is nice..." He tossed the stem on the plate then lifted the lid from the second tray. "I think I'd rather have this."

Underneath the second plate was another mound of fat strawberries, but these were dipped in chocolate then drizzled with white chocolate and dotted with chopped pistachios.

Picking one from the top, he brought it to her lips just like he had the other.

"This is all that but even better," he said. "These are coated with a layer of rich luxury, a little nutty."

She bit the end and let the smooth chocolate melt on her tongue, and when she'd swallowed the last of the bit, Marc pressed his lips to hers and tasted the essence.

"Mmm, sweet and tangy, smooth and salty. Even better, don't you think?" He gave her the rest of the berry then took one of his own.

"This is definitely more delicious," she agreed.

They sat for a moment, enjoying the treats. She hadn't noticed that next to the plates, a bottle of champagne sat buried in the ice, and Marc pulled it out and poured them two glasses. She took a sip, all the while waiting for him to explain to her where they were going and what he had in mind, and when he didn't, she finally asked.

"So, are you going to tell me how you plan to take your life and dip it in chocolate?"

"I'm selling my interest in Clearwater Springs."

She gaped. "You what?"

"I'm done having to answer to a board. I'm done working tireless hours cooped up in an office doling out investor reports and worrying about the bottom line. That's not why I went into the hospitality business." Then he grinned. "And the best part of it is I seem to have made a pretty healthy profit off my shares."

"You have a buyer for your shares?"

"I have a half dozen of them lined up." He winked. "You're looking at a pretty successful businessman."

He tapped his glass to hers and took a sip.

She could only sit and stare. "So what are you going to do?"

"The question is what are *we* going to do? And being a pretty significant life decision, I think I should get your input before I commit."

"Commit to what?"

His smile was playfully evil. "You'll have to wait and see when we get there."

She studied him, still surprised by his news but even

more touched by the fact that he actually wanted this to be something they did together. She couldn't remember a time when someone asked her what *she'd* like to do with her life. Since she was a teen, her parents had hired agents, lawyers, publicists and personal assistants, all of them constantly chattering in her ear telling her what to do and how to live her life. This was the first time she'd been asked to think for herself. And given this was Marc's life, too, the gesture meant even more.

He chuckled and brushed a tear from her cheek. "Don't worry, we'll be there soon."

She shook her head. "It's not that. I'm just… happy."

"Good. That's the way I want you to stay."

For another hour they kept driving, making easy conversation while Rachel waited in anticipation to see what Marc had planned. She phoned her mother to tell her that her trip to Italy would have to be postponed, and Marc shared with her how he'd conspired with her father to divert her plans. It was just after noon when the limo slowed and came to a stop, and Marc led Rachel out into the warm afternoon and the fragrant scent of summer blooms.

Ahead of them stood a large two-story stucco building with a red tile roof, shaded by palms, vines and decades old fruit trees. A wide brick path curved up to the colorfully tiled entrance, bordered by lush beds of shrubs, roses and flowers that trickled onto the walkway.

"Welcome to Longview Manor," Marc said. "It's not exactly the scale of Clearwater Springs, but if a man were in the market for something smaller and easier to manage, this would be an enticing prospect."

She grinned. "Enticing indeed."

Taking her hand, he led her up the path that widened

into a large front terrace. Several sets of dark wooden French doors opened to the terrace, and they stepped through the main one into what felt more like an over-size living room than a hotel lobby.

The scent of coffee and spice greeted her as she entered the space, and as her eyes adjusted to the light, she caught sight of several cozy seating areas bordered by cushy sofas, warm tapestries and elegant area rugs.

An elderly woman approached wearing a smile that was sincere and welcoming. "Marc, so good to see you." Marc took her hand and she turned her friendly eyes to Rachel. "You're Rachel Winston. I'm Helena Longview."

Her hand was bony but her handshake firm, and Rachel smiled and replied, "Nice to meet you."

"Did you have an easy time getting here?" the woman asked.

Rachel flashed back to the sex in the stretch limo and tried to hold back a blush. "Yes, it was very pleasurable."

"Good, good. So I guess Marc here is going to sell you on the place," she said. "Mr. Longview and I spent forty wonderful years here. Raised three children on these grounds. Of course, most of it was open land when we bought it, but the tourist trade has done well over the years. We've expanded about as far as we can given the acreage."

"I'd like to show her around if that's okay," Marc said.

"Absolutely." She pressed a hand to her chin. "All the rooms are booked, I'm afraid, so I can't show you any of the suites, but you're free to wander the grounds. Robert's out in the courtyards somewhere. If you need anything, I'll be manning the front desk."

"That will be perfect," he said. Then he placed his hand at the base of Rachel's spine and led her through the large room.

To their left was an upscale restaurant with an adjacent café that opened to the back courtyard. To the right, a good-size gift shop sold everything from toiletries to bestselling novels to clothing, pottery and accessories. Much like Clearwater Springs, the interior was rustic with red stone floors, cool stucco walls and dark exposed beams crisscrossing the ceiling. But this room was much smaller, more like one of her father's estates than a grand hotel.

"This main house holds the restaurant and café," Marc began. "Along with the gift shop, that's it for retail establishments. This is pretty much Longview's version of the plaza," he joked. "And it all shuts down at ten each night."

They continued through the room where he pointed to a long hallway that went off to the right. "There are eight rooms in this building, all on the ground floor. The second story is the penthouse apartment. It could be rented out, but the Longviews chose to live on-site." He looked at her and smiled. "I couldn't imagine doing anything differently, to be honest."

Stepping out into the back courtyard, they turned and looked up. "That entire second level up there is the apartment, surrounded by the private roof balcony that goes all the way around."

"It's beautiful," Rachel gushed. Turning, she studied the grounds and imagined the view the large balcony would provide.

"There's twelve acres in all."

Two single-story buildings bordered two sides of the courtyard, both with floor-to-ceiling windows that spanned the entire length. "That's the spa," Marc said, pointing to the one on the right. "Behind it is the pool and Jacuzzi." Then he pointed to the building on the left. "That's the only banquet room. They don't do corporate functions, only weddings and private parties."

"Weddings and parties?"

Marc smiled. "Yes, and Helena has always been the event coordinator here. When she and Robert sell, the new owner will need to find someone to replace her."

A lump formed in Rachel's throat as Marc took her hand and continued leading her through the courtyard. She tried to think of a more idyllic life than one living on these grounds, tending to guests and hosting beautiful parties. Granted, she'd learned from her month at Clearwater Springs there was a ton of work involved, but it was work she'd discovered a knack for, and one far more comfortable for her than standing in front of a camera posing in lingerie or trying to pretend that she could act.

"On the other side of the banquet room is a flower garden with a gazebo where they hold most of the wedding ceremonies."

Would one of those ceremonies be hers? she wondered. It was almost too much to take in all at once.

He kept walking, showing her the rest of the compound that included six suites with private terraces that opened to a grassy lawn. Then at the farthest end of the property, two single unit buildings with three bedrooms each and kitchens offered family vacationing for larger groups.

"There are only sixteen units on the property," Marc said. "Granted, they can accommodate more than a hundred guests between them all, but the Longviews said they usually run about sixty guests at a time on average.

It's too big to call a bed-and-breakfast, but not quite a full-scale hotel. But the small size offers them the luxury of a slower pace or even taking some time off when they want it. For several years now, they've closed the resort entirely for a week to go on their own vacations when they want to get away."

He stopped under the shade of a large magnolia tree and took her hands in his. "And the best part of it all is that with the money I'll make off Clearwater Springs, I can afford a big enough stake to bypass other investors altogether. I'm almost positive the financials are good enough to secure bank financing for the balance."

She cleared her throat. "I've got a little money."

"You do, do you?" He raised a brow and smiled.

She giggled. "Okay, I've got a lot."

He wrapped an arm around her shoulders and pulled her close, turning her so her back was to his chest and they could stare out over the beautiful grounds. "Are you suggesting a partnership, maybe you and I buying this place together?"

"Back in the limo, you said something about *we*."

She felt him nod against her cheek. "I did. And what do *we* think about this place?"

"It looks like paradise."

She turned to face him, and when she did, the playful look in his eyes was gone, replaced by something that looked like a man very seriously in love.

"You were right, Rachel. I was doing it all wrong."

"I never said you were doing anything wrong."

"No, but you showed me I was during those weeks we spent together." He brushed a hand across her cheek and pulled a stray strand of hair away from her face. "When I'd first set out to go into business, I never wanted to run something as big as Clearwater Springs. I'd actually looked into buying this place at the time. That's how I met the Longviews. Back then, I didn't have the kind of money I have now, and I needed to find investors. Then Brett threw his shoulder out and had to quit tennis, so the idea of a golf and tennis resort sort of blossomed from there. But it was never my dream to have so much to take care of."

He turned and looked up at the large building across the grounds. "This was always my dream, only I'd lost touch with that until you came along." He pulled her into his arms and held her close. "I want a life where I can help a lonely kid maybe see things differently, or spend a couple hours on the terrace listening to the stories of an old war veteran. I want to spend an occasional weekend on a canoe at the lake without fearing my business will collapse if I'm gone."

Cupping her face in his hands, he smiled. "Brett wants to start playing again. And like I said in the car, we keep each other real. I can't do this without you. So what do you think about us taking something like this on together?"

Snaking her arms around his neck, she closed her mouth over his and kissed him silly, wondering how many ways she could say yes. Tears stung her eyes and her heart felt as if it might explode, happiness welling and pouring over as she drank in the taste of him and tried to grasp everything he was offering.

And only when she'd lost her breath completely did she pull away and nod, afraid to open her mouth for fear of the high-pitched squeal that might come out.

He laughed. "You like this place?"

She kept nodding.

"There's another inn down the coast near San Diego, but one of the nice things about this place is it's not too far from Palm Springs. I think most of the Clearwater staff commutes from this direction. I'm thinking we might be able to steal some of the good ones."

That broke her silence. "Anita?"

"I kind of like Miguel, too, and there are a couple guys on the maintenance crew I could bring in. I'm sure for the right price we could entice the guys to make a change." He tipped her chin so her gaze met his. "I'm not in this to get rich, Rachel. I just want to spend the rest of my life in paradise with a beautiful woman who makes me happy and will keep my feet on the right track."

She grinned, not sure that it was possible to be any happier than she was at this very moment. But then she looked around and envisioned spending her life here, enjoying the people who came and went, being part of a family who would work together to make this a destination people would continue to enjoy. And most of all, spending her nights in the arms of a sexy man who loved her for who she was and who she loved back with every ounce of her heart.

"Who could ask for more than paradise?" she teased.

He smiled. "Not me."

"Me neither."

* * * * *

COMING NEXT MONTH

Available June 29, 2010

#549 BORN ON THE 4TH OF JULY
Jill Shalvis, Rhonda Nelson, Karen Foley

#550 AMBUSHED!
Vicki Lewis Thompson
Sons of Chance

#551 THE BRADDOCK BOYS: BRENT
Kimberly Raye
Love at First Bite

#552 THE TUTOR
Hope Tarr
Blaze Historicals

#553 MY FAKE FIANCÉE
Nancy Warren
Forbidden Fantasies

#554 SIMON SAYS...
Donna Kauffman
The Wrong Bed

REQUEST YOUR FREE BOOKS!

2 FREE NOVELS PLUS 2 FREE GIFTS!

HARLEQUIN *Blaze*

Red-hot reads!

YES! Please send me 2 FREE Harlequin® Blaze™ novels and my 2 FREE gifts (gifts are worth about $10). After receiving them, if I don't wish to receive any more books, I can return the shipping statement marked "cancel." If I don't cancel, I will receive 6 brand-new novels every month and be billed just $4.24 per book in the U.S. or $4.71 per book in Canada. That's a saving of at least 15% off the cover price. It's quite a bargain. Shipping and handling is just 50¢ per book.* I understand that accepting the 2 free books and gifts places me under no obligation to buy anything. I can always return a shipment and cancel at any time. Even if I never buy another book, the two free books and gifts are mine to keep forever.

151/351 HDN E5LS

Name _____ (PLEASE PRINT)

Address _____ Apt. #

City _____ State/Prov. _____ Zip/Postal Code

Signature (if under 18, a parent or guardian must sign)

Mail to the Harlequin Reader Service:
IN U.S.A.: P.O. Box 1867, Buffalo, NY 14240-1867
IN CANADA: P.O. Box 609, Fort Erie, Ontario L2A 5X3

Not valid for current subscribers to Harlequin Blaze books.

Want to try two free books from another line?
Call 1-800-873-8635 or visit www.morefreebooks.com.

* Terms and prices subject to change without notice. Prices do not include applicable taxes. N.Y. residents add applicable sales tax. Canadian residents will be charged applicable provincial taxes and GST. Offer not valid in Quebec. This offer is limited to one order per household. All orders subject to approval. Credit or debit balances in a customer's account(s) may be offset by any other outstanding balance owed by or to the customer. Please allow 4 to 6 weeks for delivery. Offer available while quantities last.

Your Privacy: Harlequin Books is committed to protecting your privacy. Our Privacy Policy is available online at www.eHarlequin.com or upon request from the Reader Service. From time to time we make our lists of customers available to reputable third parties who may have a product or service of interest to you. If you would prefer we not share your name and address, please check here. ☐

Help us get it right—We strive for accurate, respectful and relevant communications. To clarify or modify your communication preferences, visit us at www.ReaderService.com/consumerschoice.

HB10R

HARLEQUIN®

A Romance

FOR EVERY MOOD™

Spotlight on

Heart & Home

Heartwarming romances
where love can happen
right when you least expect it.

See the next page to enjoy a sneak peek
from Silhouette Special Edition®,
a Heart and Home series.

Introducing McFARLANE'S PERFECT BRIDE
by USA TODAY bestselling author Christine Rimmer,
from Silhouette Special Edition®.

Entranced. Captivated. Enchanted.

Connor sat across the table from Tori Jones and couldn't help thinking that those words exactly described what effect the small-town schoolteacher had on him. He might as well stop trying to tell himself he wasn't interested. He was powerfully drawn to her.

Clearly, he should have dated more when he was younger.

There had been a couple of other women since Jennifer had walked out on him. But he had never been entranced. Or captivated. Or enchanted.

Until now.

He wanted her—*her,* Tori Jones, in particular. Not just someone suitably attractive and well-bred, as Jennifer had been. Not just someone sophisticated, sexually exciting and discreet, which pretty much described the two women he'd dated after his marriage crashed and burned.

It came to him that he...he *liked* this woman. And that was new to him. He liked her quick wit, her wisdom and her big heart. He liked the passion in her voice when she talked about things she believed in.

He liked *her.* And suddenly it mattered all out of proportion that she might like him, too.

Was he losing it? He couldn't help but wonder. Was he cracking under the strain—of the soured economy, the McFarlane House setbacks, his divorce, the scary changes in his son? Of the changes he'd decided he needed to make in his life and himself?

Strangely, right then, on his first date with Tori Jones, he didn't care if he just might be going over the edge. He was having a great time—having *fun*, of all things—and he didn't want it to end.

Is Connor finally able to admit his feelings to Tori, and are they reciprocated?
Find out in MCFARLANE'S PERFECT BRIDE
by USA TODAY bestselling author Christine Rimmer.
Available July 2010,
only from Silhouette Special Edition®.

HARLEQUIN *Presents*

Bestselling Harlequin Presents® author

Penny Jordan

brings you an exciting new trilogy…

Needed:
THE WORLD'S MOST ELIGIBLE BILLIONAIRES

Three penniless sisters:
how far will they go to save the ones they love?

Lizzie, Charley and Ruby refuse to drown in their debts.
And three of the richest, most ruthless men in the world
are about to enter their lives. Pure, proud but penniless,
how far will these sisters go to save the ones they love?

Look out for

Lizzie's story—**THE WEALTHY GREEK'S CONTRACT WIFE, July**

Charley's story—**THE ITALIAN DUKE'S VIRGIN MISTRESS, August**

Ruby's story—**MARRIAGE: TO CLAIM HIS TWINS, September**

www.eHarlequin.com

HP12927